For Melanie
with best wi

ONLY THE DANCE

Anthony

ACH SMITH

V. '22

◆Tangent Books

Only The Dance
First published 2021 by Tangent Books

Tangent Books
Unit 5.16 Paintworks, Bristol BS4 3EH
0117 972 0645
www.tangentbooks.co.uk
richard@tangentbooks.co.uk

ISBN 978-1-914345-13-5

Author: ACH Smith

Cover design: Jaz Naish

Publisher: Richard Jones

Assistant Publisher: Sol Wilkinson

Production: Joe Burt

A CIP record of this book is available at the British Library.

Set in Garamond Pro 10.5/15

Printed on paper from a sustainable source by TJ Books in Cornwall

ACH Smith is the author of a dozen novels. They include two previous thrillers, published by Weidenfeld & Nicolson, The Jericho Gun ("Unputdownable" – Sunday Times) and Extra Cover, featuring the characters of Charley and Mike, who are pleased to reappear in Only The Dance.

Much of his fiction has been set in Bristol, where he has lived since the 1960s. His stage work and screenplays include Up the Feeder, Down the 'Mouth (1997, revived 2001), a celebration of the days when Bristol Harbour was still a working port. It broke the Bristol Old Vic box-office record. More recently, the subject of Walking The Chains was Clifton Suspension Bridge.

He has also published poetry, and several books of non-fiction, including a memoir, Wordsmith (Redcliffe Press, 2012). Among some 200 TV programmes he has written and presented was The Newcomers, directed for the BBC by John Boorman, a portrait of Bristol in the 1960s. He has been Cilcennin Fellow in Drama, University of Bristol; writer-in-residence at the University of Texas; director, Cheltenham Festival of Literature. A full list of his work can be found on his website, www.achsmith.co.uk

1

THE FIRST THREE go down, but Johnson brings the fourth one home at 7/2 and Charley collects ninety quid from Jerry Evans. "You'll spend it all at once," the bookie says, "so I won't tell you not to."

Charley shrugs. "Sixty of it's what I did in on the races before, so ten quid up on the day. It'll be hard not to spend that all at once. You seen what they charge for a pint here?"

"Wasn't sixty in my satchel, though, was it?"

"Not at the prices you were showing."

"Gotta round my book, Charley. You know that."

He does know it. He'd even clerked for Jerry one day, a few years back, when it was still pencil and columns and the usual clerk had gone missing. The usual clerk, Henry, was now 78 years old. He liked telling people he'd been clerking at Epsom for some old bookie when Sea Bird won the 1965 Derby. "It was beautiful to see. We had a pitch second row in Tatts, so up on the step I had a perfect view. I knew it was going to drain the joint dry, but – I've never seen anything more beautiful than that. Never forgotten it. Two lengths, on the bridle. I dare say Nijinsky was something to see a few years later, but by then I'd moved down here."

Charley once asked him, "Fifty-odd years in the game, what changes have you seen in all that time, Henry?"

"None at all. Nothing's changed."

And Charley at once recognised the truth in that. It is why he, and everyone else, loves it. Electronic boards now, sure, and computerised books. but still the cocktail of raucous and county, greed and perilous grace. Mike had always been there with him, all the years since they'd left school, but he still can't fathom how Charley squares his Labour vote with gambling. "It's easy," Charley once explained. "I won't treat money like holy shit. It's Tories who revere money." But Mike had shaken his head, none the wiser.

After the last, walking back to where Mike's van was parked, Charley knows where the conversation will turn, and here it comes. "You're forever moaning about being broke, but whose fault is it? It's twenty years since we left school, and you still haven't found yourself a proper, signed-up job. You've got brains, Charley, you know you have, more brains than I've got, but what do you use them for?"

"I read books."

"You read books. In preparation for what?"

"That's not why I read."

"It should be."

"In preparation for settling down with someone, you mean? Getting a mortgage? You remember what Zorba the Greek says in that film we saw. 'Wife, children, house – the full catastrophe.' Great line."

"Great line when Anthony Quinn says it, but a pile of tosh when you give it a moment's thought."

"Quinn must have given it more than a moment."

"He's an actor, Charley. He's faking it."

"Me too. All the time. Do you ever get that feeling?"

"He made a lot of money faking it. But you – "

Beside the kerb a stout man with a jacked-up BMW is struggling with a wheel brace, cussing it.

"You want a hand?" Charley asks.

"Bloody thing won't shift."

Charley takes the brace and gives it a shove and nothing moves. Then he stands back and kicks it. With a squeal the nut turns.

"You're a legend, sir", the man says.

Mike remarks, "I've skinned my ankle doing that before now."

"Yeah," Charley says. "I remember you missing a penalty in a match at school. It's not that you didn't score, you just missed the ball. It hadn't moved."

"It was a feint. Ref should have let me take it again."

"Nah, you just kicked air. There's a delay on the line between brain and foot."

"Can I give you a lift when I've fixed it?" the man asks.

"No, thanks," Mike replies. "We're just walking to where I left my BMW."

"Well, call it two pints if we ever bump into each other again."

"No worries," Charley says.

Mike adds, "Cheers, drive."

"Ah, you're from Bristol?"

"Yeah, Horfield," Mike tells him.

"Off Whiteladies," Charley says.

"Right. I'm in St Werburgh's. Might see you in the Old England. The name's Randolph. Randolph Wheen."

They exchange names, shake hands, and walk on. Mike says, "There's nothing wrong with my brain-to-foot co-ordination. It's not like your brain-to-brain disconnect."

Mike's old Citroën van smells of cooking oil. With the side flap up he earns a living serving snacks around the Horsefair. "I'm in the catering industry," he tells people and, when he hears that, Charley tells them, "Yeah, he's got two Michelin stars, Mike has. He's after his third one with the way he has with deep-fried grasshoppers." Men smirk, women say "Eurrghh." Mike looks to one side, sniffs, and says nothing.

He drops Charley on Blackboy Hill. Charley is very careful to close the front door quietly but it's no use. His landlord, on the ground floor, is waiting with the door of his room open. "Charley," he calls. "You're two days late with your rent."

Charley spreads his hands.

"Again."

"You know how it is with the IMF. They never come across on the due date."

"Then you'd best fly over to Washington and tell them you'll be sleeping in a cardboard box on the pavement if I don't get it by the end of the week. And you haven't even got a mangy dog on a string to keep you company."

In his room, Charley puts a frozen pizza in the microwave, and goes online to study tomorrow's card at Newbury. He won't get there to enjoy it but he can nip out to the shop when he takes a break from painting a bedroom for an old lady in Cotham. She'll pay him sixty-five quid in his back pocket, and with what he's got left from today all he'd need to pay his rent is one decent winner. And she's a nice old biddy and might be able to point him to a friend of hers who needs a bit of painting done, or a dripping tap re-washering, or a cat or a budgie to be taken over to the vet, or a few hours in the garden, the allotment, whatever. He can turn his hand to all sorts, and there are plenty of old people around here who need all sorts.

****

The Chinese lot are in the shop today, talking at the top of their voices. They always do. It must be noisy in their country.

In the juvenile hurdle there are three unbeaten in their races to date. He goes for the one trained by Hobbs, stable in form, second-rated by the Racing Post. It gets beaten two lengths by one that has never raced before. Charley slowly crumples his betting slip into a ball and tosses it toward the plastic-topped table. It lands clean in the green bin beside it. Every time he gets that right he feels his luck has turned. He's in control. Perched on a stool, elbows on the ledge, chin in his hands, he studies the form for the next race, pinned up on the wall.

Steve the ambulance driver joins him. "How's your luck?"

"I wouldn't know," Charley answers. "I haven't seen her for some time. Not sure I'd recognise her if she came in that door whirling tassels on her tits."

"Mike told me you had a nice winner when you were over in Chepstow with him."

"Yeah, but five nice losers to go with it. By the end I reckon Mike would have been ahead of me with his little two quid fav and third fav about forecasts."

"Know anything today?"

"Steve…" Charley grins silently at him for the hundredth time in response to the same enquiry. every day.

Steve grins back. "Would you tell me? Of course you wouldn't. But you know, I've never understood that about you, Charley boy. Why you'd withhold a scrap of almost certainly duff info from a mate."

"I don't want the responsibility of seeing you lose."

Steve shakes his head. "It's not that. Can't be. You put us all on Dear Katya in the Gold Cup, each way at twelves, when you were on that big roll."

"Yeah, that ended well, didn't it?"

"She came in third. We all collected."

"I mean, how it ended for me. Five weeks in a ward at Frenchay."

"You were both up to something then, weren't you?"

"Can we talk about something else?"

"How about the winner of the next race?"

To halt the loop, Charley peers closely at the form, and Steve walks away, with a sigh. For a minute, Charley isn't thinking about the horses but about the kernel of truth in what Steve said, his reluctance to share any clues. He is not sure he understands it himself. Was it genetically inherited from a neolithic forebear who might come across a patch of succulent blueberries and want to keep them secret for his own family in the cave? How can he square that with the convictions in which he had been brought up by parents who had themselves been brought up in the postwar welfare state, the blessed generation?

It is not that he has any ripe insights to share about Hexham's two-mile handicap chase, next on the card in front of him. In the trainers-in-form table he's noted that Bailey has reappeared after a quiet spell, and it's a long way to send a no-hoper from Gloucestershire to Northumberland. He writes out a £5 win slip at

6/1 and hands it to Pam behind the counter. She puts it through the machine and the horse unseats its rider at the fourth. So it goes. The Chinese sound as though they got the winner, but how can you be sure about the constant noise they make?

He walks back to the half-painted bedroom off Blackboy Hill twenty pounds shorter of his rent. He can give his landlord what he's got left on account, and find the balance next week. Find it somewhere.

2

ON THURSDAY IN the hall there is an unstamped envelope with his name on it in blue ink. The note inside invites him for a pint at the Old England on Monday evening at 8.30. It is signed Randolph Wheen. He has to think, then remembers: the bloke with the punctured BMW. Well, why not?

"How did you find my address?"

"The electoral roll," Wheen tells him. "It wasn't hard. There wouldn't be many people called Charles Midsomer living near Whiteladies Road."

"You'd have to know how Midsomer is spelled."

"I'd have settled for the other spelling. What are you drinking?"

Charley asks for a pale ale, which they've got on tap. Wheen brings it to the table, with a gin and tonic for himself. He is a short man, in chinos and a dark blue blazer, a crisp green shirt with white stripes, polished brown shoes. When he talks, in a voice drawling down at the end of a sentence, he makes more eye-contact than Charley is comfortable with, but he has a ready smile.

"That's a Gloucestershire badge on your jacket."

"Yes," Wheen says. "I'm a member there."

"Do you play the game?"

"I used to, when I was at school, Colston's. But now, the old legs, you know?"

"Yes, I know. You bat with your feet."

"You do, yes. You play yourself?"

"Now and then, when somebody asks. I'm not in a team, not any more."

"What do you do, bat, bowl?

"I bat. But what I'm best at is grabber. Round the corner, snatching them up. I love it when we've got a good off-spinner in the side. If I wasn't sure about playing, that would tip it."

"I'll remember that if I'm ever asked to raise an invitation eleven. You'd have been in your element for Gloucestershire when we had David Allen and John Mortimore, both of them at the same time. They grew up together at school, you know. Cotham Grammar. And Arthur Milton was there too. What a school team they had."

"And, you know, that same school produced Paul Dirac and Peter Higgs."

Wheen shakes his head. "Who did they play for?"

"They were particle physicists."

"Ah. Not my field."

"Another thing – Paul Dirac was at Bishop Road Primary with Cary Grant."

"That's a name I do know."

"Not then you wouldn't. He was called Archibald Leach as a kid."

"You'd do well in a pub quiz, wouldn't you? How do you know all this stuff?"

"I read books."

Wheen nods. "And you follow the horses?"

"How do you know about me and the horses?"

"I see you with a Racing Post stuck in your coat pocket walking away from Chepstow racecourse with your buddy at five-thirty on a Monday afternoon, I don't need Dr Watson's help, do I? You're clearly a gentleman of leisure."

"The leisure bit's right. In-between odd jobs."

"And that is exactly why I asked you to meet here. I have a proposition for you. But first, I want to thank you for your help last week. Cheers."

They take a drink. "A proposition?" Charley asks.

"That's right. Deliveries."

Charley rolls his eyes to the ceiling. "Riding a bike through the traffic with a big box of pizzas on my back? Mister…"

Wheen waves his hands. "No, no. Driving. You can drive?"

"I can drive. I haven't got a car, though."

"That doesn't matter. A car would be supplied. You've seen it, the BMW."

"That's a delivery car?"

"Yes. It's not mine. It's for delivering luxury goods, to high-end customers."

"Lacy bras and panties?"

"No, no. Caviar, Swiss liqueur chocolates, that kind of thing."

"Where, in Bristol?"

"Sometimes, yes, but all over – Cotswolds, Mendips, Wiltshire, Devon coast, Cornwall even."

"This is your business?"

"No. It's run by a friend of mine. I've been doing the deliveries for her, but I was nabbed for drink-and-drive the other day, and they told me at the station that I'll be facing 20 months suspension when it comes to court. That's the usual tariff. I want to help her out by finding someone to take over from me. She wouldn't know where to start looking."

"She found you."

Wheen shakes his head. "No, her husband did. He and I were pals. It was his business, but he died suddenly, a year or so ago, so I've been helping his widow to keep the business going. But now I've made this balls-up, and…" He gestures at Charley. "What do you say?"

"Why me?"

"I'd already started to scratch my head about where to look for someone when I meet you, quite by accident, and I think, hey, he might fit the bill."

"What bill is that?"

"Personable manner. A bit of nous" – Wheen taps his skull – "for dealing with customers, though there's seldom any trouble, they're county people, professionals, that type. So, someone needing work but with spare time. It's not every day, maybe three or four deliveries most weeks, it varies. You'd be paid £100 per delivery, irrespective of how long the drive is, but with a guaranteed weekly retainer of £400. How does it sound?"

How it sounds to Charley is like Jingle Bells every week, but neolithic man keeps his cards close and his face straight. "This boss of yours – a woman, you say?"

"She's called Elira. Elira Richardson. Lives in Kingsdown, over there. You'll like her. She's a generous employer."

"But will she like me?"

"That's the judgment I'm making. That's why I wanted this meeting."

"I'm being interviewed."

"Head-hunted, I'd call it. But of course, next thing will be that you meet her, and then it will be her decision."

"You don't mind if I say – it feels a bit odd? I'm a stranger to you. I might be Jack the Ripper. There's no-one you know better you might have asked?"

"Oh, I know lots of people, naturally, at the cricket club, neighbours, old school friends, pals from when I was working as a solicitor. But everyone who came to mind has other commitments, jobs, family. Are you married?"

"No."

"So you'd be freely available? Odd jobs wouldn't get in the way?"

"That could be arranged."

"Excellent." Wheen stands up. "Another pint? To – can't say, seal the deal, that's up to Elira, but I feel confident. As you must do when you pick your horse."

"Ha!" Charley exclaims, with the sarcasm stop full out. Then he nods. "I won't say no. Thank you."

While Wheen is back at the bar, Charley decides he can't tap him for an advance, to pay his rent. It wouldn't look businesslike. He'll just have to string his landlord along with the promise that he's about to nail a regular income.

****

Two days later he meets Wheen by appointment at three p.m. outside the pub, and they take the short walk up to Kingsdown. "Will Mrs Richardson be wanting references?" he asks.

Wheen shakes his head. "Just my recommendation will do."

"I've been thinking – tell me, how will you manage without

this income?"

"Good of you to think of it, but no worries, as they say in Sydney. I took an early pension from the law firm I used to work for, and my wife has a little income from a herbal medicine practice she runs. And we bought our house in the days when they were still affordable. We're comfortable. I did the job for Elira to help her out, that's all. I was very good friends with her late husband, Jack. We worked together, at the law firm, Arthur Podger, you know?, in Stoke Bishop. All four of us used to meet for supper quite often."

"He died, you said?"

"Yes, poor chap. Heart attack. No-one saw it coming. He was out playing golf every weekend. I'd play a round with him occasionally. And then – just like that. Dreadful shock. Don't mention him to Elira, she's still getting over it. And she has a teenage daughter to bring up. But the good thing is, she's always done the book-keeping for their business, so was well placed to take it on."

"And you won't struggle without the car?"

"Oh no, I've got my own car. Not quite as grand as the Beamer, but that belongs to the business. I never used it privately. Nor will you."

He stops outside a tall Georgian house. "Here we are."

3

ELIRA OPENS THE door and takes them to her sitting-room. Charley is glad he had made the effort to dress as smartly as his wardrobe allowed, jacket and tie and suede shoes. In his everyday gear he would have felt even more uncomfortable among the period furniture, paintings framed on the wall, small grand piano, very shiny, two filled book-cases, big potted plants (a yucca he recognised from gardening), all beige carpeted, fancy spotlights, and a dark red chaise-longue on which Elira perched, motioning the men to deep armchairs upholstered in brown leather.

"Charley?" she asks, with a smile, "or Charles, for now?" Her voice has a slight hoarseness.

"Charley is fine. I might make it to Charles if I ever get married." He is wondering if the butler will be entering with crumpets and Lapsang Souchong.

"Charley, right. Randolph tells me you could be available to do some deliveries for me."

"That's right, I'd be interested." He is pleased with himself for interested.

She lays it out as Wheen had told him. Car provided, three or four deliveries a week, five or six occasionally, some of them local but mostly across the West Country. "And we have one or two clients over in Wales. How does all that sound to you?"

"I could manage all that."

"Good. I'd pay you £80 per delivery, with a minimum weekly guarantee of £320 as a retainer."

Charley glances at Wheen. "Er, Mr Wheen told me it would be £100 per delivery and £400 retainer."

She also glances at Wheen. "It's not for Mr Wheen to set the terms of our agreement. Eighty and three-twenty is what I'm offering."

It's almost as many Jingle Bells, but Charley doesn't want to come on like a pushover. Presumably Wheen's numbers were what he had been getting himself, but then, he is an old family friend. "How about ninety and three-sixty?"

"Eighty and three-twenty." She is not smiling. Her face is lovely, meticulously made-up, but she is not smiling. While Charley considers his position, she adds, "This is not a deal-breaker, surely?"

He nods. "Okay."

"Good. We don't need a formal contract. You have my word, and a solicitor there as witness." Her glance now at Wheen is cold. "I'll pay you in cash every Friday. Can you start tomorrow?"

"I can. What time?"

"Be here at 10 a.m. please. Tomorrow it's just one delivery, to Radstock. Now, let me show you the car."

Charley wishes Wheen had said something, to oil the discussion, but the man had sat there impassive, while Elira, in her grey silk pencil-style shift, has held the room like the leading lady.

He goes downstairs with her. Wheen stays on in the sitting-room.

There are two gleaming BMWs in the garage, the dark blue one that Wheen had been in at Chepstow, and a black one. Charley notices the plates. The black one has a registration from last year, the blue one is five years old. Elira opens its door. "You've got satnav, and I'll always give you the client's postcode, so it will find the best way for you. You know how to key in satnav?"

"I've never used it, no."

"No problem." She shows him. "And for the return journey you just press this button and say 'Take me home', and it will show you the route back here. When you need to fill up, keep the receipt for me and I'll reimburse you."

"Do I collect payment for the deliveries?"

"No, no, everything is done online, orders and invoiced payments. Drive and deliver, that's all there is for you to do. And get a signature for delivery. Have you driven a BMW before?"

"No, but I've rented other swish cars in my time, so I'll soon get used to the works. I'm glad to see it's a stick shift. I prefer the control that gives you."

"I understand." She smiles. "Well, 10 a.m. tomorrow."

"See you then."

****

See You Then. It was Charley's favourite farewell, after the horse had won its third Champion Hurdle for him, Steve Smith Eccles up. At 16/1 the first win, what an evening that had been, and me just a teenager. What a trainer, Nicky Henderson. The horse had legs of glass. But after all, the trophy had been sponsored by Waterford Crystal. See You Then...

He is whistling as he walks home, then changes his mind and heads down to the Horsefair. Mike needs to hear about this.

"Eighty quid for driving to Radstock and back? That's 40

minutes each way, you're raking in a quid a minute. Taxi drivers don't earn that rate. I was pitched outside Ashton Gate for the match last night, four hours I was there, took home 31 quid. Call it 15 after supplies and expenses. Fifteen quid for four hours. And you – "

"It was raining. People didn't want to hang about."

"No, specially not after what they'd just seen on the pitch. I should have been selling pistols for them to shoot themselves. If I had been they'd have shot wide. What is it you're delivering that the Man can pay you that? If it's pizzas they must be sticking on one hell of a mark-up."

"It's not a man, it's a woman. She's selling luxury goods. Caviar, and that."

"Caviar, eh? But dodgy that, Charley. They've been over-fishing it in the Black Sea, so I read. I think they've made it illegal now."

"So I'm risking being caught in possession of caviar? It would sound glam in the papers. Make me a star."

"Who is she, this woman?"

"She's a widow, bit older than me. But in good shape, a dresser, blonde hair down to here, and she's got that indentation under her philtrum that always turns me on."

"Under her what?"

"Her philtrum. Oh come on, Mike, I've told you this before. It's this." He strokes his philtrum. "This little cleft below your nose that we used to think was a snot channel when we were at school. In some women it makes their top lip into a shape you just – well, it's called a Cupid's bow. Know what I mean?"

"Charley mate, this money she's paying you, it's gone to your head. Or maybe not your head."

"Oh no, you've got it wrong. I'm not going to get ideas. She's a very professional woman and talks like one. She's out of my class."

"What class is that?"

"Not my mark. I was simply offering you a dispassionate appreciation of what it is in a woman that might be attractive. I should have known better, talking to someone like you."

"I'm not someone like me. There is no-one like me."

A pair of teenage boys are ordering hamburgers from Mike, and Charley leaves him to it. He'll buy fish and chips on his way home, and then give his landlord the good news and enjoy watching the man's face.

4

10 A.M. SHARP. Elira gives him the car keys and a parcel the size of a shoe box, wrapped in gilt paper, unlabelled. "I'll put it in the boot here, for security, so make sure the boot is safely locked if you stop for any reason." She hands him a slip of paper with a name and address on it. "Keep this separate from the parcel, get it signed for receipt, put it in a safe pocket, and make quite sure to return it to me, all right? This is vital, Charley, for book-keeping. And my clients expect perfect confidentiality and don't want their addresses floating around like dandelion seeds. When you get back, ring the bell and I'll be down to open up the garage door and collect the keys and receipt from you. Or my daughter Roze can do it if she's back from school and I'm busy. Okay?"

"Sounds simple enough."

"It is. Keep it simple. Have a good trip."

He does. The sun is shining, the car is a beautiful drive, down St Michael's Hill, round the Bearpit to Temple Way, past Temple Meads, Wells Road, not much traffic now, through Pensford, with a toot for Acker, to Farrington Gurney, left to Radstock, the satnav takes him to a quiet country lane. He checks the address on the receipt, spots the house, standing in its own grounds with a drive, takes the parcel from the boot, and rings the bell. Though bulky, the parcel weighs little. A young man opens the door, takes the delivery with a nod, signs the receipt, and Charley is back in Kingsdown just before noon. Simple.

Elira answers the bell and invites him in. "You got the signature?" He brings the receipt from his top pocket. "Good. Would you like a drink?"

Sitting in the armchair he had sat on before, sipping Talisker from a crystal tumbler, he asks, "Anything tomorrow?"

"Nothing tomorrow, Friday, so I'll settle with you now. We agreed £80 a trip, but since it's a short week to start you off, here's £100."

She is more relaxed today. Maybe it was a household fret yesterday, but more likely Wheen's silent presence had unsettled her, for some reason Charley can't guess, nor probe.

But she soon resolves it for him. "I wanted the chance to know you a little better, with Randolph out of the way. The trouble is, he's an old friend of my late husband, and he does like to think he knows my business better than I do. It's often the way with solicitors. But he's misguided. It depends absolutely on getting and keeping the right client list, and ours was built up first by Jack, my husband, and it's sustained now by me."

"How do you do it, find the right clients?"

"Most of them come via word of mouth. One satisfied client might introduce one or two more. But I have found clients myself, just by keeping my ear to the ground."

"You've still kept a shapely ear."

She ignores his clumsy compliment. She has no interest in flirting with him. "For instance, I'm keen on Scottish dancing, I go every week. And that's the sort of milieu where you are likely to find clients, just through casual conversations. You'd be surprised whose hand you might find yourself holding in an eightsome reel.

It depends where you are, of course. Whereabouts in the country, I mean, There's high end at Scottish dancing, like everywhere else. I've danced with a Russian oligarch. I'm not going to tell you his name, but you might recognise it."

"Does he own a football club?"

"I didn't ask."

"I would have."

"But you wouldn't have been holding his hand."

"I'm bound to wonder – but tell me to keep my nose out of it if you like – to wonder what it is I'm delivering that gives you the margin to pay me well."

"I don't mind telling you. It's all luxury goods. My speciality is caviar, when I can source it. It's not always easy. In particular, there's white Beluga, from Iran mostly. At trade rates I have to pay several hundred pounds an ounce, so you can imagine what the client price will be. Now and then I'm offered wild caviar, which costs even more, because of the legal controls. But there are people out there, if you know them…"

"Russian oligarchs."

"Yes, if you can find one. In Russia they're used to these luxuries, so they're pleased when someone like me can supply them. But there are American people too, and a few British, bankers, people of that sort. Of course, they could go to Harrods or Fortnums for most of what they want – truffles, old single malt whiskies, speciality chocolates, perfumes, fashion accessories – but what they get from me is a select private service, with recommendations if they ask me, at the door when they want it, no fuss. Sometimes at short notice, when suddenly they're having a party, and want to impress their guests. I know how to source high end, how to lay hands on what

I want. So they're happy to pay for it. And I can pay you, and keep my daughter at her school, and look after the house."

Charley is thinking, info overload. He wanted a conversation, not a presentation. Why is she so keen to dish out all the details of her business? He's just the driver. But he holds his tongue, nods understandingly, crinkles the five £20 notes in his pocket, and accepts a refill of the whisky, noting that she is knocking it back as eagerly as he is.

A telephone rings in another room. While she is answering it, he looks more carefully at the furnishings. He gazes at the portrait in oils of a young woman in a blue dress, and stands up closer to it. No connoisseur, he thinks he can read the signature. When she returns, he turns from the painting and asks her, "Is that signature 'Manet'?"

"Yes."

"Is it the original? The real thing?"

"Yes. Do you like it?"

"It's lovely, but I never expected to see a real Manet in a Bristol drawing-room."

"Why not? I've got a good security set-up here."

"I'm glad to hear it. It must be worth a few bob."

"I've never had it valued. It was a present to me from my husband. He bought it at Christie's. I'd feel a bit materialistic finding out how much he'd spent on me."

"Did he come from a wealthy background, your husband?"

"Not particularly. He was at Clifton College, and then trained as a solicitor. That's how he became a friend of Randolph Wheen. They worked together."

"Mr Wheen was at Colston's School, he told me."

"Was he? I wouldn't know."

"I thought he might have mentioned it. He says he and his wife were family friends of yours."

"His wife? I never met a wife. I've got a vague idea that he might have been married when he was much younger, but it didn't last. He's always been a single man in my experience. He's got no offspring, that I know of. Lives alone, somewhere over St Andrew's way. Why on earth would he be spinning a yarn like that to you?"

Charley shrugs. "I can't answer that. I've only had one proper conversation with him."

She was shaking her head. "He did some deliveries for us since we started the business, three or four years ago, and just occasionally Jack would bring him up for a drink, like you and me now. That's as far as it ever went. Family friends? No."

From her tone of voice, Charley reads the subtext: I can do better for friends than someone like Randolph Wheen.

He says, "It was the act of a friend to find somebody to take over the deliveries for you, when he had to stand down."

"It was the least he could do, not leaving me in the lurch. I'm vulnerable, as a single woman."

You don't look vulnerable, Charley thinks. On the chaise-longue she is poised on one haunch, profiled, a leg crossed away from him, her glass held idly in a hand stretched along the backrest. How many whiskies had she had before he got back? That slightly hoarse voice of hers, and the angle of her head, are all signalling a professional distance, and he will respect it, but he can't help wondering. Wondering about her, but about himself too. He's never been with a woman perhaps ten years older than he is, who smiles only in politeness, and hasn't yet made a joke of any kind.

Wondering what she'd make of it if he came out with one of the quotes that infest his mind like brainworms. "Imagination was given to man to compensate him for what he is not, and a sense of humour was provided to console him for what he is." He'd have to start with something like, As Sir Francis Bacon said, and she would probably find it simply weird, or pitifully pretentious. Maybe it's only the whisky at work, but stirring somewhere in him is a feeling for her like sympathy. A sense that she is lonely in her widowhood, and her brisk, strictly professional conversation is a defensive mask. "Vulnerable" might have been the right word after all. Mightn't it?

"So," she says, "nothing till Monday. There are two booked for Monday, and it's a bit of a drive, Calne, then Glastonbury, or the other way round if you like, up to you. After that, there's one on Wednesday, near Bath, easy."

She's telling him to push off now. "Okay," he responds. "Ten o'clock?"

"Ten o'clock will be good."

He walks home feeling happy. He's got some allotment work tomorrow, helping an old bloke who can't bend down any more, the horses on Saturday, and Sunday there'll be a match he can watch in the pub. Up with the pace on his rent, and a book about Russian history he's just started to read. It's time the sun broke through those clouds again.

5

CHELTENHAM IS HIS favourite course. Everyone's favourite course, isn't it? When God created the earth He thought, hold on, they'll be needing a perfect racecourse, so He scooped out a natural arena for them in the Cotswolds, and then invented the Irish people to bring over a piquant green flavouring to it, not just in March. Charley once asked Paddy (generic names save time), "Tell me something. For years here at the Festival I'd see two or three Catholic Fathers in their full togs, black cassock, hat with things dangling. There was one every year, a very fat man, and I once watched while his right hand went under the left side of his cassock and brought out the Sporting Life open at the form page, and his left hand went under the other side and came out with a bottle of John Powers's Gold Label and raised it to his lips. It almost converted me. But these last few years they've been missing. Has the Church changed its attitude to gambling?"

"No, no," Paddy had said. "They've nothing against it, never did have."

"So long as you find the winner," said his friend Seamus.

"And", Paddy added, "put some of it in the plate next Sunday."

Today, for the International Hurdle, Charley fancies Smudger's Hope. Mike is doubtful. "It might do it in the big one, come March, but this is its first run since May, it's just being tuned up, and to see whether it likes the course and will come up the hill.

Cross it off for today."

"The stable's in good form, twenty-three per cent winners."

"And so is Mullins, and he doesn't send them over from County Carlow to enjoy the view of Cleeve Hill. Galway Masters is your banker. It won by lengths three weeks ago."

"Beating what?"

"You can only beat what you meet."

"Could be a song there." Charley improvised a tuneless tune. "You can only beat what you meet. A day without a flutter is toast without butter. You've gotta have a punt, or else…" He stopped it there, demurely.

"Flutter away if you want. You've got it to burn with this new job of yours."

"Mike, if I clear three-twenty a week, that's still only about sixteen grand-odd a year, which is some way shy of the national average. Not much to burn there, after food and rent."

"Come on, you've got your odd jobs too. You told me, you won't be working for her every hour of every day."

"Which is why I've got the pleasure of your company today. They're going down. I want to find sixes about Smudger's Hope."

He plunges into the jungle of the ring. His pick is actually 13/2 on most boards, which pleases him because three of the tipsters in the paper have gone for it. Then he spots 7/1, and tramples old ladies to get his £20 note in the bookie's hand. That's how it is in the popular ring at Cheltenham, though old ladies are thin on the ground. They'd gone to Kempton for the King George VI, and were shocked to find that in the suburbs of London people form an orderly queue to get their bet on, which invariably meant that by the time you reached the bookie he'd rubbed out the price you were after and brought it in a point. That's not gambling, it's buying a pig in a poke. Better to poke a pig. They grin when you do it. Fact.

He watched Mullins's horse bring Walsh up the hill to win by a length, and endured Mike's shouting it home. He never did that. It's fine and arguably dandy to back the winner, and to feel you've out-shrewded the bookie, which is as good a feeling as the money you collect, but you celebrate with a stoical, calm dignity, because you know it's not going to happen repeatedly. For this half-hour you have been blessed. It will be followed by another half-hour.

Mike is saying, "I did it to win and in the forecast with that thing, the one in pink and black, it did hold on for second, didn't it?" The result is announced and yes, Mike goes to the Tote window to collect about £16. He bets in two-pound coins. Saves them from his takings on the van. In spite of the triumphalist shouting, Charley is pleased for him. He opens the paper and starts to study the next race.

****

"There's some funny things about it I don't understand," he tells Mike in the van on their way home. "For one thing, she keeps changing the number plates on the car."

"That's illegal."

"I know, but that's not what bothers me. The thing is, why does she do it? I've been driving for her for four weeks now, and I reckon I've had half a dozen different plates."

"She must think someone might be snooping."

"Snooping on what?"

"The clients you're delivering to. It could be business sense, to mislead competitors."

"Competitors? In the caviar and truffle trade? It can't be a jungle out there."

"You'd be surprised. I had a fish-and-chip van marauding on my pitch last week."

"Another thing is that bloke Randolph Wheen. You know, the one we gave a hand to at Chepstow with his car, the car I'm driving now, and he recruited me for the job with her. He fed me this line about him and his wife being great family friends with her and her old man who died, and now she tells me that's bollocks. And he hasn't even got a wife. Who do I believe?"

"You believe ten different tipsters in the Racing Post every morning, it's not that much of a stretch, is it?"

"Yeah, but by the end of the day we know if one of them was right, but I've got no way of knowing which of these two is having me on."

"Does it matter? Enjoy ambiguity, that's my motto."

"Is it? I've often wondered what your motto was."

"If you don't trust it, I've got others."

Charley smiles. "No, it does matter. Trust, that's exactly the problem. I feel as though I'm some kind of toy they're playing with. There's some history between them, I can tell, and they're working it out with me as the shuttlecock."

"You say he hasn't got a wife. Maybe he had a thing with her, if she's a looker, like you say. And he dumped her, or she gave him the heave-ho, whichever."

"Maybe. That would account for the coolness between them. And, I wonder, he could be lying about why he's not driving for her any more, some story he gave me about being caught drunk in charge, he seems to tell a lie whenever it suits him, and the truth is he just didn't want to see her any more. That would figure. By George, you may have cracked it, Watson."

"A simple logical deduction. Logic, that's what you should be thinking about, Charley. Not all this history you're into. What's the point of history? You can't go back and change it."

"No, but it can come back and change you."

"I don't understand you."

"Nor do I."

Mike is changing down to negotiate the roundabout at Cribb's Causeway.

"I heard this bloke on the radio," Charley says, and puts on a lofty tone. "History is the black sheep uncle whose debts I repudiate."

"The programmes you listen to," Mike chuckles. "Try Tony Blackburn. He gets me through a long rainy evening on the Horsefair."

"And good on him for that. But you know me, Mike. I'm trying to catch up with what I didn't get at school."

"And what good is that going to do for you? Get you some cushy number in an office, because you can come up with a quote you heard on the radio?"

"That's not why I do it. You know it isn't."

Mike does know that. He will never endorse it but he respects his old friend's struggle. He just wants to shield him from the disappointment in store. Lionel Bart got it wrong. Fings are what they used to be, always will be.

6

IT'S AN EARLY start, a two-hour drive to Totnes. When he rings Elira's bell it is answered by a teenage girl in smart school uniform, crested blazer and tie. "Hello," she says, "you must be Charley."

He nods. "I guess I must be."

"I'm Roze, Elira's daughter. She's just getting ready to take me to school. Here, she gave me the parcel and the car keys for you, and the address slip."

"Why is it that girls are always giving me the slip?" he asks. She laughs, and he likes her, a girl who gets his joke. "Thanks." He looks at the slip. The address is Dene Manor, near Totnes.

"I'll open the garage for you. Have a nice drive. Wish I were driving to Devon on a lovely sunny day. Instead, I've got double biology. Urgh."

"Tell you what, you take the car to Totnes and I'll go and do the biology for you. The bilge we used to call it when I was at school."

"Oh, I wish..." she says. "Ojalá. That's a word I learned in Spanish last week. It means, 'I wish', or 'would that.'" She says it again, enjoying it, with the guttural j, "Ojalá, Ojalá. It's followed by the subjunctive. Do you know about the subjunctive?"

"Would that I did."

"Very good." She laughs again. "You don't speak Spanish, do you?"

"I'm afraid not. Ojalá."

"I love it at school. But that may be because Mr Street, who teaches us Spanish, is young and dishy. Not like Mrs Hawes, who takes us for biology."

"You have a nice day," Charley bids her, and puts the parcel in the boot. It's always the same parcel, shoebox size, wrapped in gilt paper with a pink ribbon around it. He is thinking better of Elira, that she has brought up a daughter that bright with a stranger.

He punches in the postcode but at first disregards the satnav direction via Bedminster, preferring the view from the Suspension Bridge. Then it's along to Portbury, where Pat Murphy used to train a small string of horses, and join the motorway south. He always smiles at the breast-shaped hill, near Bridgwater. A reclining goddess of the Mendips. Full of history and myth and legend, this wetland area of Somerset, Bronze Age barrows in the limestone, Joseph of Arimathea, Roman lead mines, King Arthur, and the Battle of Sedgemoor, and the Witch of Wookey Hole. Years ago a girl had brought him one winter's day to skate on Priddy Pool, but he'd never done it before and his ankles couldn't get the hang of it.

Dene Manor is what he expected, a mansion, Jacobean he guesses, standing in open ground with a wood behind it. He parks beside a Merc, takes out the parcel, and pulls a chain by the front door that rings a loud bell inside. A woman in an apron answers it, but he can tell from her voice that she is not a maid but the lady of the house, busy in the kitchen, perhaps getting ready for an evening with guests and caviar. "Come in, come in," she says. He's not used to being invited in, but welcomes a break.

She takes him to the kitchen and he puts the parcel on the big wooden table. "From Elira," he says.

She frowns. "Another one? But we had a delivery from her,

when was it?, two days ago I think it was."

"From Elira, in Bristol?"

"Yes. We always buy from her."

He shakes his head. "You sure?"

"Quite sure."

"But I'm her delivery man, and I wasn't here two days ago."

"I'm sure you're right, but I didn't take that delivery, my sister answered the door because I was in the bath."

"But it was definitely from Elira?"

"Yes. My sister brought me the receipt to sign. My husband's on a business trip in the Turks and Caicos, so I'm looking after things."

"Maybe your husband sent Elira two orders."

"Not likely. It's always one every few weeks. He'd have told me otherwise."

"It must have been some different company delivering something."

"No. I opened it, and it was just what we've always had on order from Elira. You're new, aren't you? Her delivery man used to be someone called Randolph. Maybe it was him two days ago?"

He looks at the parcel he has left on the table. "Did it look like this one, the one he left, whoever he was?"

"Pretty much. It's how Elira always wraps them, isn't it? I can't swear it had a pink ribbon like this one, I don't remember, and it's gone now, yesterday was the day the bin men come."

Charley is sitting with his elbows on his knees, staring at the table. "Well, there's been some mistake, obviously. But would you like this extra delivery anyway?"

"I'm sorry, I can't take a decision like that without my husband.

It's quite a price, you know."

He nods. He does know.

She says, "You've come all this way and it's a wild goose. I'm sorry. Would you like a cup of tea?"

"Thank you. It's kind of you."

"Not at all, not at all. At least it's a lovely day for a drive."

A door on the far side of the kitchen opens and a young man in pyjamas and a silk dressing-gown comes in, stretching his shoulders. "Oh, Adrian, you're up at last," the lady says. "This is my son Adrian. He's a night bird. Adrian, this is Elira's new delivery man, Charley. I'm sorry, I should have introduced myself. I'm Eleanor. Eleanor Duxford."

Adrian looks at the parcel. "It's from Elira, in Bristol? Another one?"

"Yes," Eleanor says, and would have started to explain that there must have been some misunderstanding, but Adrian is already asking, "And your name's Charley?"

"That's right."

A smile on Adrian's face turns into laughter.

"What's so funny?" Eleanor asks him.

"If you don't get it I'm not going to explain."

"Adrian, dear, Charley could think you rude to laugh at his name."

"I'm sorry, I'm sorry, I didn't mean to be rude. It's just so – "

"So what?"

"Nothing, nothing. Is there a cup of tea going?" He has got his laughter under control.

Charley is sipping his tea. A light-bulb at the back of his brain has switched on, and is getting bright.

Adrian makes conversation, no doubt to varnish over his faux pas. He asks Charley where he lives in Bristol, and says he knows Whiteladies Road well because he's in his second year at Bristol University, but his digs are in Cotham. He's doing a law degree but expects he will wind up in accountancy, because his father works in finance and will find an opening for him. He doesn't ask Charley anything about himself because, obvs, Charley is a delivery driver, enough said. He leaves his empty cup on the table and excuses himself. He's at a crucial point in a game of Stronghold Kingdoms on his computer and has to get back to it before the other players take advantage. He might bump into Charley one day when he's over that way. He leaves with a waved hand. "Ciao."

Eleanor looks at Charley, her eyebrows raised to say, what can you expect from teenagers?

He picks up the parcel, thanks her for her hospitality, and drives back past Newton Abbot racecourse, then passing near the Exeter track, to join the M5, then north. He is trying to think what the duplicate delivery could mean. Is his job at risk? Is Elira shunting him into the sidings? But she wouldn't have let him go pointlessly all the way to Totnes. Hold on, he hadn't seen her this morning. But she'd sent her daughter down with the keys and stuff. Is some other firm trying to muscle in? Would it be best to hide the parcel and say nothing about it to Elira, hoping that what's happened was a one-off freak? No, her accounting will alert her that she's not been paid. And she'll want the signed receipt. He thinks about forging a signature on it. Receipt, deceit – what happened to the p?, it is there in deception... He recognises the game his mind is playing, a game of elusion, not wanting to concentrate on what really matters right now. What matters is that deceit would incriminate him, and he

40

has committed no crime. The only thing for it is to tell her what has happened, no fault of his. But that laughing boy has unnerved him.

He won't open the parcel until he gets back to his place.

7

HE IS CAREFUL in removing the ribbon and unfolding the gilt paper because he would rather Elira didn't know he has been snooping.

When he lifts the lid of the sturdy cardboard box, what he sees, laid out on purple tissue paper, is two half bottles of Château d'Yquem, 1989 vintage; two tins of caviar, identifiable by a picture on the tin-lid, surrounded by script in what might be Arabic; and a small wooden crate of Belgian liqueur chocolates.

He's asked Mike to come over, to help him assess what he finds. "What is that lot going to set you back?" Charley wonders.

Mike shrugs. "The chocolates, not a lot, twenty, twenty-five quid, but the other things – I don't know about wine vintages, but top of the market could be five hundred the pair of bottles. And the caviar – I checked before I came and it ranges from maybe thirty quid a very small tin of bog-standard that you'd give your butler for Christmas to, well, you can pay thousands for state of the art. Which I don't mind betting this is, with no English name on the tin, and they're big tins."

Charley is sitting back in his chair, gazing at the box. Then he realises that the box is deeper than the bottles laid on their side. What they can see is a top layer. He looks and sees the edges of the layer, takes the bottles off, and removes the shelf. Below it are four plastic bags of small, white powdery rocks. He grunts, in recognition of what he'd been expecting. He's never seen it before, but everybody knows what it looks like. "Blow, snow, coke," he says, "Big C for Charley! Chaaarleee!" He laughs.

"Jeez," Mike says, "you're a county line."

"She might have told me."

"You're a county line for posh county cokeheads. No wonder she's paying you well."

"Right. Would she pay the fine when I get caught?"

"On the street I've heard it's forty quid a gram. How many grams there, would you say?"

Charley takes the four bags and weighs them in his hand. "A wild guess – maybe half the weight of a four-ounce bar of chocolate, two ounces, say. What's that in grams?"

"Um, something like fifty grams."

"Fifty times forty makes two thousand."

"At street price. She'll have paid the dealer maybe half that, so a cool grand margin."

"Or more. The kind of Hooray Hedgies I'm delivering to wouldn't blink at double the street price. They're not going to buy baggies in back alleys."

"That's her USP. She's running a toff-licence."

Charley nods. "She might have told me."

"What are you going to do?"

"Tell her I know. Tell her she should've told me."

"And quit?"

Charley thinks. "If I did quit it would be on principle. Her false pretences."

"And not paying you enough for the risk you're taking for her."

'Maybe. It's the deceit that hurts. I can't pretend I've got any moral problem with the stuff. It should have been decriminalised years ago, like they've done in Portugal I heard."

"But that was about heroin injection, and getting HIV from the needles."

"Was it? Smack's different, it's a killer. I wouldn't carry that for her, whatever she was paying."

"I wouldn't touch this stuff."

"Nor me. I've got an addictive personality, I know that. But delivering it, I don't feel any grubbier about it than if I was delivering gin."

"I hope the judge will share your lenient view."

"I'd remind his honour that Sherlock Holmes used it. Those prim people in Victorian times didn't think it criminal."

As they re-wrap the parcel, trying to restore it to a tidy condition, Charley tells Mike about what else is on his mind, the duplicate delivery. "I just can't figure out where the other one might have come from."

"It could be an error in her order book," Mike suggests.

"No, that would mean she's using another delivery driver. without telling me. Why would she do that?"

"She's a devious dame. She didn't tell you what you were delivering, did she? She's got a lot of good cards and she's keeping them all very close to her chest. Where you'd like to be."

Charley shakes his head. "I don't think it's that. For one thing, we've been getting on pretty well, her and me. What would be the point of not telling me? Plus, she's not the sort to make an error in the book. She's an impressive businesswoman."

"Then the only other explanation is that the people in Totnes use more than one supplier, and they forgot they'd already ordered from someone else."

"Mmm. They said they always bought from Elira. They know how she wraps things, like this one."

"There could be a rival supplier elbowing in."

"How would they know about the order?"

"They've hacked her email?"

Charley nods slowly. "That would figure. Yes. I'll alert her when I see her. But she might have some other explanation we haven't come up with."

"Right," Mike says. "I've done enough unloading of what's on your mind. Let's go for a pint."

"I can't. I've got to get this stuff back to her. I might see you later, when I've straightened it all out with her."

****

He rings the bell, Elira opens the door and sees him holding the parcel. "What happened?" she asks. "Couldn't you find the house?"

"It's more complicated than that."

They go up to the sitting-room and he tells her what happened in Totnes. She sits quietly for a minute. He waits, then says, "You haven't got another driver working for you, have you?"

"No." She is quiet.

"Then I reckon you've got a rival on your patch. And maybe they're hacking your computer to check out your order book."

"I've got maximum security on my computer. I paid a specialist to shield it. And all the payments go to a bank in Geneva." She shakes her head. "How could anyone break into that?"

"There are some clever dudes out there, in places like Moscow or Skopje or Lagos."

"How would people in places like that know about my business?"

Charley pauses. "Well, that's the other thing I wanted to ask you about. When this happened in Totnes, there was a kid there who laughed when he heard I was called Charley, and – I'm sorry, but that clued me up about what might be inside the parcel so I took a look. You should have told me what I was carrying for you."

"I did. Luxury goods."

"Oh yes. Luxury goods that could land me in the slammer if the fuzz caught me."

"The cocaine, you mean?"

"The cocaine, I mean."

"I thought you'd have figured that out for yourself weeks ago. How else could I be paying you like I do?"

"Well, I didn't figure it. Not till now. You should have given me the choice. I feel exploited."

She might have answered sarcastically, oh poor little innocent Charley, how could I exploit diddums?, but she doesn't. She's better than that. "I didn't tell you because I knew you'd guess, and we'd both feel more comfortable with a tacit, grown-up understanding. I was banking on your being streetwise. And not snitching."

He thinks about that, and has to recognise that he feels flattered. He says, "This is exactly the kind of business that the clever dudes out there are very interested in knowing about."

"That is what is worrying me," Elira says.

"It should."

"Look," she says, "I'll level with you."

"I'd like that."

"I was born in Montenegro, in a little Albanian enclave there, on the coast of the Adriatic. My mother was Montenegrin. That's why my daughter's name Roze is spelled with a z, that's how they spell it there. My own name, Elira, is Albanian. My father was English. He met my mother when he was over there working for the British Council. I grew up in this country, I've got a British passport, but I've got Albanian cousins who have moved here, to London. It's through them I source the cocaine. They've got some deal with Italians who bring it across from Antwerp, in containers I think. They trust me, my cousins, but there are other people in that business there who are greedy and would like to carve off my niche for themselves. And they are not nice people. You understand?"

Charley nods.

"And that's what is worrying me. I thought I had camouflage of a sort, with the other goods I sell, caviar and so on, not the sort of stuff people like that deal in, but my fear is that if they know I have a line in cocaine they'll want it for themselves. They want the high-end client list I've built up, with my husband till a couple of years ago. They'd struggle to make connections of that sort themselves, but if they could rip off my trade, ready-made... You see?"

Charley nods again. "Well, if you've been hacked, there's your suspects."

"I'd be dumbfounded if I have been."

"Better shielded people than you have been found dumb. Big companies, the government..."

"And how would they get payment? These people in Totnes, they don't pay cash in hand."

"I can't tell you. I didn't think to ask. The not nice lot could have hacked your bank account, too."

"In Switzerland?"

"You're right. If they got into your account they'd just have taken the money without needing to deliver anything. But – hold on, they could switch the account number to one of their own, so that new cash just goes through to them without touching the sides."

"I'll ring the bank tomorrow and make sure nothing fishy has been going on. Oh god, I could do without this. I've not been sleeping well as it is."

"Let's hope it's a one-off and we'll laugh when we realise something daft went wrong."

She shrugs, not convinced. "These people… There's a violent streak in the Albanian culture, you know. They've got a word kanun. K a n u n. You pronounce it like the biblical name Canaan. It means a blood feud. You must have revenge, even years later. And the worst are the ones who've been coming out of Kosovo, after the troubles there, you know?"

"I read about it."

"Some of them have got themselves over to London, and they're the ones upsetting what used to be an orderly business. Illegal, sure, but there's honour among illegals, and respect for how things are done. But now, it's especially the young ones. All they're interested in is getting a Ferrari and a gold Rolex. They had pretty drab lives before, but when they see what you can get in London, it drives them insane. Insane."

Charley stood up. "Well, we'll see. Fingers crossed. When's my next delivery?"

"Thursday. Okay?"

"I'll be here."

As he was leaving, she said, "Oh, by the way, I've got a favour to ask you. Thursday evening, after you get back, would you come with me to Scottish dancing?"

"Elira, I haven't got the knees to wear a kilt."

"You don't have to wear a kilt. Only a few of the older men do. But the trouble is, we're always short of men, and most of those who do come are older, and we're always trying to recruit younger men, to balance out the numbers."

"I can't… I've seen it on telly but I wouldn't have a clue about the steps."

"You don't have to worry about that. We have a beginners section, to take you through one or two easy formations to start with. You'll soon pick them up. And the rest of the time you can just sit there with a glass of beer and enjoy the spectacle. It's quite something to see, you know."

"I dare say, but…"

"Please, Charley. I need something to look forward to, after what we've just been talking about."

"Well…"

"I'll buy your beer for you."

8

MIKE CAN'T STOP laughing. "You, Scottish dancing?"

"Och aye."

"I don't think there's much scope for smooching, from what I've seen of it."

"That's not the point."

"What is the point?"

"Boss's orders."

"Hoots mon, oot o' ma way, who do you think you arrrrrr?"

"It's an old Bing Crosby number, isn't it?"

"It's the toe o' ma boot, mon, if you step too farrrrr."

"I'm expecting something more dignified than that."

"Charley, after twenty-odd years with the horses do you still believe there could be any connection between what you expect and what happens in the finishing straight?"

"I'm up today. Ain't I, Pam?" he shouts to the counter.

"Ain't you what?" she answers.

"Up. Today."

"Well, you're out of bed, if that's what you mean."

"On my betting is what I mean."

"I really couldn't tell you, Charley," Pam says. "I takes the money, I pays out the money, I'm not keeping personalised accounts for every customer."

"Why don't you put your lips where your mouth is, darling?"

He is up, by £22, thanks to a neat little hurdler at Cartmel. Always the same, he thinks, you do okay when you've already got a few notes in your back pocket. Some version of Sod's Law.

Mike won't let it go, his jokes about jigs and reels. "It'll be more like pigs and squeals when you're doing it. I wish I could be there to watch you trying to pick it up."

"You're never too old to learn something useless," Charley says.

"Well, I've got to get back to my van. Those hamburgers won't eat themselves."

"They might eat each other, by the look of them."

"That's a thought. Cannibal hamburgers. I might chalk that up on the board. Could shift a few." As he stands up, Mike's elbow knocks a half-drunk plastic mug of tea over his trousers. He swears, and starts to mop himself with a handkerchief.

"It might have been worse," Charley says.

"How?"

"You might have knocked it over me."

They leave the shop together and walk down Whiteladies Road. "You know," Charley says, "the politically correct lot would have us believe that Whiteladies is some sort of old racist name. It's not. It got its name from a nunnery that used to be over there, where the artillery ground is now."

"All very well, but what about Blackboy Hill, up the top?"

"Another misconception. It was named for an old inn up there called the Black Boy, which was a popular nickname for Charles II, on account of his hair. There used to be a picture of him painted on the inn sign. There's a book in the library with an old engraving showing it."

"What a lot you've got stored in your noddle."

"Yeah, most of it fascinating and useless. It's like someone's old loft in here." Charley taps his head. "There's a book I came across, by an American writer. His grandfather was one of those people who could never throw anything away. When the day the family had been dreading came and grandfather died, they had to go in and clear his house. Up in the loft there were masses of big cardboard boxes, all carefully labelled. One box was filled to the brim with tiny bits of string, an inch long. It was labelled, String Too Short to be Saved. That's what it's like inside my head."

"You need to look for someone who could help you have a clear-out."

"A shrink, you mean?"

"Maybe. Or one of these mindfulness gurus you read about."

"I've already got a mind full. That is the problem."

"Okay, how about Buddhist chanting? Om… Om…"

"That might work."

"Or one of those Albanians you say your boss is bothered about. They'll clear your head in no time if you come up against one of them."

Charley nods. "But she can't be sure it was them, this duplicate delivery in Totnes."

"You got a better solution?"

"No, it's a mystery."

"Live with it. The world's full of mysteries. You just have to live with them. It's what makes life enjoyable. We'd all die of boredom without a few unsolved mysteries."

"But what if it happens again?"

"Her problem, not yours."

"If I agree with you we'll both be wrong."

****

He spends half the evening in the church hall sitting at a table, with a glass of pale ale, just watching, nervous about when it will be time for him to stand up. It is not unenjoyable to watch. The repeating patterns working themselves out give him a geometric satisfaction. The steps the best dancers take, with poised ankles, are as elegant as herons. The tunes, played from a CD box through speakers, are cheerful. "On special evenings we have a piper," Elira tells him. She doesn't miss a dance. He admires how straight her back is, how precisely on the beat her feet. She is fit. Is she high, on her luxury goods?

After half an hour most of the dancers take a break, and a group of three beginners, two young women and Charley, are incorporated with five of the regulars. Elira takes charge, first walking them through the formations, showing them how to rise on their toes and keep their heads erect. They go through the formations twice more, then someone switches on a CD for them. It is of course faster than they are ready for, there are mistakes in the formation, syncopated shoes, stumbling, collisions, but enough smiling and laughter to keep it going without terminal embarrassment. Elira is patient and encouraging. She allows them a minute's break, then runs them through it twice more. She claps her hands and all the dancers come back to the floor and join the beginners for one more performance of the same reel.

Charley takes a break. A young woman with long auburn hair and – for chrissakes – blue eyes is sitting alone at a table. That's the seat for him. He buys a beer at the serving hatch and puts it on the table. "Would you like one?" he asks her.

She shakes her head. "I'm fine," she says.

"I can see you're fine, but would you like a drink?"

She hesitates, then says, "An orange squash?"

He gets it for her, and takes a mouthful of beer. "Are you a regular?"

"When I'm free. My parents, over there, bring me."

"What are you up to when you're not free?"

"I work at a stable."

"You're a jockey?"

"No, no, it's a riding stable, near Thornbury. I teach kids to ride. I do ride myself, show-jumping."

"I think you might be the woman I've been looking for all my life. You know about horses. I know about betting on them, but I've always wanted somebody knowledgeable to watch them in the parade ring and tell me which one is really up for it."

"Oh, I couldn't do that. I don't like racing. It's cruel to the horses."

"They never get hurt show-jumping?"

"It can happen, and it's horrible when it does, but it's never because we're whipping them to go faster or take a huge fence when they're tired. We don't have whips."

"I quite agree that it's horrible when one comes down. You should hear how quiet the crowd goes. We clap when it gets up again. We love them as much as you do. They are beautiful. But a racehorse would not exist if it weren't for racing. That's why they're bred. Ask yourself this: you are a stallion's seed and I offer you the choice. Either you will fertilise an egg and grow up to be strong and gleaming and athletic and live the life of Riley, groomed and fed and medically cared for and pampered rotten, lots of Polo mints, and all that's expected of you in return is that just a few times a year, for a few years, you do something that quite possibly, how can we know?, you really enjoy because it's natural to you, race against other horses, with a minute risk, one in a hundred, that you might fall over and if you do, and you're not just winded but badly hurt, you are swiftly put out of your pain, but almost certainly you'll wind up in a long and comfortable retirement in a green pasture. All that is one choice, or – you will not be born. Which would you choose?"

"But," she answers, "the horses I work with get all that without running the risk. Or hardly."

"Okay. But – in the world, around 100,000 thoroughbreds are foaled every year, but that number would be much, much smaller without racehorse breeding."

"Just so that you can have a bet."

She is dodging Charley's logic but he doesn't tell her so. Instead, he says, "My name's Charley."

"And mine is Charlotte."

"It was written in the stars that we should meet."

"Or in the register of births. Where were you born?"

"Here, in Bristol."

"So was I. Well, Almondsbury, not far. What do you do for a living?"

"I make sure to stay alive."

Her shyness is easing, slowly. She smiles for the first time, and takes a sip of her squash. Another dance has started, and they have to talk more loudly.

"Mostly I do deliveries, but a bit of decorating and gardening on the side."

"Who do you deliver for?"

"For Elira, over there, who was teaching me the steps. It's my first time at this."

"Oh, I know Elira. She's always here. Did you find it difficult, first time?"

"You bet I did. But fun."

"Good. You'll be coming again?"

That's a promising question. "Maybe." He won't get her to the races, so this place is his best hope.

"What's her line, that you deliver?"

"Luxury goods. Caviar, that kind of thing."

"Mmm, I love caviar."

"She sources it from Albania, as far as I can make out. She was born over there, she told me, so she's got the connections. All I knew before about Albania is that when they ran out of kings, about a century ago, they tried to get C.B.Fry to do the job for them. He was an English cricketer."

"How extraordinary. And he wouldn't?"

"No. Pity. He'd have introduced them to cricket and we'd be playing Test matches against Albania. Instead, I read, they crowned some chap called Zog. You wouldn't call a strip-cartoon character Zog. Would you?"

"I wouldn't know. I don't read strip cartoons."

"And Zog didn't go down well with the Albanians. They showed their disapproval of him by trying to assassinate him. Repeatedly. There were so many assassination attempts that he put his mother in charge of the palace kitchens to make sure they couldn't poison him."

"How do you know all this?"

"I read a lot, when I'm not delivering, or painting."

"All I knew about Albania till now is that they used to have a harsh Communist régime."

"Yeah. It's a shame. Someone should give Communism a proper try."

She puts her finger to her lips. "Don't let my father hear you say that. He'd have you assassinated."

Well, she was born in Almondsbury, what did he expect? "The Diggers did give it a go, in Surrey," he says, "but Cromwell was not having it. So we might guess that your father would hit if off with Cromwell."

"Oh, I doubt that. He's a staunch royalist. God save the Queen, and all that. He still stands for the national anthem. There can't be many left who do that."

"And you, dear Charlotte, where do you stand in all that?"

"Well, I'm not a Daddy's girl, if that's what you're asking."

"No, what I'm asking is whether there's any chance I might see you again some time."

Before she can reply, another jig starts up. "Excuse me," she says, "they'll want me to join in," and she does.

And when the jig finishes she has disappeared, and he can't find her again the rest of the evening, and he has not even got her 'phone number. He would have to come Scottish dancing again.

Driving him home, Elira says, "I've got a special job for you on Sunday. Can you do that?"

"Sure."

"I need you to drive to London for me and collect some goods. I'd do it myself, but it needs to be in the evening, you won't be back till midnight, and I'm not sleeping well and I could fall asleep at the wheel, and I have to be up early to get Roze to school."

9

EVEN IN A BMW, it's the same motorway tedium. Bath, Chippenham (he smiles when he remembers Jezza in a battledress jacket coming into the betting shop after a long absence, probably in the slammer, and saying "I've just got back from 'Nam," and someone exclaimed "Vietnam!?" and Jezza replied, "Nah, Chipp'nam."), Swindon, Newbury... If he were going to Newbury races it would be different, but Elira has sent him to Barking. She's given him a woolly hat to wear which will be recognised by the bloke he's got to meet in a pub, but it's an Aston Villa hat, claret and sky blue, and Charley points out that he risks being beaten up in Barking by some Orient nutter who hates West Ham, but she shrugged and said, "I've already told him what to look for, so it's too late to worry about that," and she punched in the satnav postcode for the Three Crowns in Barking. "His name is Zamir. It's all paid for," she tells him. "You've just got to collect, and bring it back here."

Reading, Maidenhead... Headlights on now. When this ends he's still got half the M25 to get round, and the traffic getting into Barking, then all the way back again to Bristol. Classic FM doesn't do it for him, he reverts to thinking about Charlotte. Was she escaping after he'd hit on her? Quite gently hit. She's surely old enough, 27 maybe, and pretty enough to be used to it. Probably there is a boyfriend in the background, a husband even, someone who owns a horse. He'll find out about that if she turns up again, hasn't been terminally turned off. If it was something else, that she had to leave pronto, Daddy was getting his keys out and saying it was time to go home, she might have found a moment to come over and say Goodnight, even if it had been nothing more than an orange squash. She must have taken fright. If so, that's probably game over. But he can't get her off his mind. It is for want of trying. He's got to think about something and he likes thinking about her. He's recently come across a new word, limerence, he can't imagine ever getting to use it, but it means obsessive thoughts and fantasies about somebody, so he can use it to himself, now, to instruct himself about what's going on in his mind while he drives, and drives... Overtaking lorry after lorry, jeez, it must be worse for them, it's all they do, day after day, he's got two days off after this, Elira told him.

Bristol's funny like that, you come across plenty of posh people but there's no shortage of artful dodgers, like Jezza, and Bemmies like me and Mike, and probably it's the same in other places, Liverpool, Newcastle, but in Bristol there's no hiding it, all the gorgeous Georgian terraces looking out over what used to be streets of miners and dockers and tobacco shredders, never far between anywhere, a city-sized village. Drive for twenty minutes in any direction and you're looking at cows.

Classy dames, he says to the dashboard in his Philip Marlowe voice, oh yes, there's been a few. He could get off with them, even if he was always wondering if he was no more than the traditional bit of rough, rite of passage, before you walk up the aisle with your father beside you in a morning suit. There had been Jacquetta, and even better (Even better, Jacquetta, why hadn't he come up with that one when he was with her?), before her there had been Jo, who knew about horses, knew a lot, and loved the races, but it was on account of her that he had wound up in Frenchay Hospital for weeks. When he'd told Mike what had happened, in a Cheltenham hotel bed with Jo, caught by her boyfriend, Mike had said "You should have reported him to the stewards for excessive use of the whip," and Charley had answered, "That's in bad taste, and so was the hospital doctor when he told me I should think myself lucky, if the bloke had been half an inch more accurate with it I'd be listed as a gelding."

But, but. She had said, "I'm not a Daddy's girl." Surely that was some sort of a wink at him? A sliver of light? Or a trick of the light? A lick of the trite? A conventional, insincere cover-up? He would like very much to find out, and meanwhile it's Slough coming up, Windsor Castle on the horizon, and onto the M25 orbital, urgh. Yes, he'd admitted once to Mike, I ought to find a nice Bristol girl from an ordinary background, there's lots of them, it can't be that hard, especially when I'm in work, but there's something about girls like Jo and Jacquetta that raises my pulse rate. You're not going to understand me, but I think it's that my natural, healthy libido gets cross-wired with my socialist beliefs and I'm wanting to make a political point in bed with them.

"You've got one thing right," Mike had said, "I don't understand you."

****

He buys himself a half-pint of pale ale and sits at a small round table, with the woolly hat on. Across the bar three teenage lads are joking around together at another table, and even yards away he can see that they are heavy with bling. All in studded leather jackets and black jeans, with rings flashing from their fingers, more glints from metalwork around their ears, mouths and necks, and big, flashy watches. He would bet that more would be revealed if they lifted their silky shirts.

One of them is staring at him, then comes over to his table, and asks, "You looking?" He's got a smear of blood on a tooth.

Charley replies, "Just taking it all in. I've never been in here before. Nice place you've got."

"No. You looking? You get me?"

"I'm not looking for anything. I'm waiting for someone. Your name's not Zamir, is it?"

The lad ignores the question. "You shouldn't be sticking around here. Where you from?"

"Bristol."

"Get back there. Advice. No charge."

"I'm going back tonight, after I've met someone in here."

"If you're not from around here, why're you wearing a Hammers hat?"

"It's not Hammers, it's Villa. Look, there's a badge." He takes the hat off and shows him the badge.

"I don't know fuck about football, but my mate over there clocked you for a Hammer. He might not be happy either about – what is it, you said?"

"Aston Villa."

"Where's that, then?"

"Birmingham."

"You said Bristol."

"I live in Bristol, but the hat's from Birmingham."

"Why?"

Charley shrugs. "A friend gave it to me."

"Fuck off back to Bristol. Right?" He stares into Charley's eyes for a few moments, then returns to his friends.

Ten long minutes pass. Charley wishes he hadn't got here on time. He could do with a double whisky, but no, he has to drive back soon, Elira wouldn't want to lose another driver on a drink charge. Then a middle-aged man in a dark suit comes in and sits down next to him. "For Elira?" he asks, with what Charley assumes must be an Albanian accent.

"Yes. Zamir?"

The man nods. "Zamir." No handshake is offered. "Come, I show you where we go."

There is no conversation as Charley follows him across the busy street, down a side road, and round the back of a slabby concrete block of many flats, twelve storeys high, with connecting walkways. Zamir presses the button for a lift, but nothing happens. "Never working," he says, "we have to go on stairs."

Starting the fourth flight, Charley says, "Must keep you fit if the lift's never working."

"I not come here every day."

"Ah, you live somewhere else."

"My house is in Potters Bar. This place, my storeroom."

On the eighth floor they go along an unswept passage and Zamir uses three keys to unlock a door. Inside, the room is unfurnished, uninhabited. He unlocks a steel cabinet, brings out a Tesco bag with a package in it and hands it to Charley. "For Elira," he says. "Good lady. You tell her, Zamir sends her his heart."

"I will. Thank you."

"Your car, where you left it?"

"In the car park behind the pub."

"I come with you." He adds, "Better safe than sorry," and smiles, proud to have learned the phrase. "You new from Elira. Was a more small man before."

"Randolph."

"Randolph, yes."

"It's me now, Charley."

"Charley, okay."

He is glad to have Zamir's company when they reach the car park. The three bling lads are there. To his relief they are not interested in his BMW. They are larking around a red Ferrari. He says, "Those three weren't pleased to see me in the pub."

"Pah! Fucking youngers. Too many of them. Too many. We don't need so many like them. The police see them behave like that, is not good, it makes us – attention, is that the right word?"

"Attention, yes."

"When they are men they will be better. But now, they know nothing. Nothing." He gestures helplessness, then waves his hands dismissively at the lads, and shouts something at them in their own language. They run back into the pub, giggling.

The bag with the parcel weighs about four pounds. Charley puts it in the car boot, locks it, and shakes hands goodbye.

"Goodbye," Zamir says. "You take care, huh?"

All the way back the bling lad's departing long stare is coming through the windscreen.

10

IT IS PAST midnight when he is welcomed by the sulphurous yellow clouds reflecting the street lighting of Bristol. He has done over 300 miles, and it is too late to deliver the parcel to Elira. He parks in the street, and will remember to move it before the 9 a.m. parking curfew. He dare not leave the parcel in the boot. Cars here are regularly duffed up by kids who have spent the evening drinking in joints on the Whiteladies strip. He carries the parcel up to his room, and is asleep in five minutes.

He doesn't know the answer to the Totnes mystery. He doesn't know if he'll see Charlotte again, or whether she'd be pleased. He doesn't know if he can trust Elira. He doesn't know what will win the Champion Hurdle, or how robins use quantum entanglement to find their way home, or whether he's got any butter left for toast in the morning, continue to end of chapter what he doesn't know. What he does know is that he never wants to meet the bling lads again. If Elira sends him back to the toxic bubble of London he will ask her to arrange for Zamir to meet him somewhere they won't be. There must be a quiet church in Barking.

He is in time to catch Elira and give her the parcel before she takes Roze to school. "Wait till I get back," she says, "I want to hear how it went yesterday."

She gets back and he tells her. She nods. "Zamir's a good friend. In my business I need good friends, and to know who they are. Jack always said, a good friend is a better investment than any insurance policy." She shrugs.

"I'm sorry about Jack, but you're doing a fine job for him with your daughter. She's a great kid. She gets my jokes."

"Ah, I didn't know you made jokes."

She grins, and so does he. The day is starting well. Well, better than yesterday finished.

"When Jack went, it was such a shock," she says. "Out of the blue, a heart attack. On the golf course, on a Saturday morning. Randolph Wheen was there with him when it happened. I find him a difficult man, but he and Jack were close. They worked together at a solicitor's. And they'd both finished there together, before it happened. I never really understood why, but there was some kind of massive kerfuffle at the firm, something to do with fake signatures on wills, and they were the fall guys, held responsible for whatever it was, and the senior partner had them both struck off by the Law Society. Officially banned from law work, you know? Not just there but anywhere else, too. Gordon McFinn had done his best to intervene on their behalf – the father of that girl you were talking to at the dance, you know?, Gordon, he's a partner at the firm – but the senior partner wouldn't listen. I'm convinced it led eventually to poor Jack's heart attack. He'd hardly ever had a day's illness."

Charley is thinking, when he gets home he will tot up how many lies Wheen has told him. Here was another one, he hadn't retired with a pension but had been sacked, for some shady business. Along with Jack, poor Jack. What had they been up to at the firm? Did Elira know, really, but was she playing the middle-class tune of gliding over the dark notes?

"Charley," she says, "I am worrying. I am worrying a lot. After that Totnes mix-up, I checked through my order book, and what I found is that several of my regular clients have gone missing lately. And of those still ordering, a couple have restricted their order to just regular goods, caviar, chocolates, you know what I'm saying?"

"I get you."

"Of course, in any business you do get fluctuations, but just lately it has looked like more than that. More than people dying, or moving away."

"Or kicking the habit?"

"That's pretty rare."

"I've been mystified myself about what happened in Totnes. I wish I'd quizzed them more, but the husband who placed the orders was away. Do you want me to look into it for you? A bit of market research?"

"How could you do that?"

"Well, how about I call on one of the discontinued clients, and see what I can get out of them? Are they dissatisfied with the product?"

"That might seem a bit hard sell."

"It doesn't need to. I'd be polite."

She thinks about it, then says, "Well, I suppose, if you don't ask you don't get answers."

"Right. Tell me the addresses of the lapsed ones."

She fetches her order book. "Um, Dursley... Burnham-on-Sea... Devizes... Bedminster..."

"I'll try Dursley for starters." He has had an idea.

"Okay. It's not one you've been to for me. Number 2, Chaddesleigh Crescent. The client's name is Kip Rawsthorne."

"I'll go tomorrow. Maybe I should take something for them as compliments from the supplier?"

"Good thinking." She checks the order book again and goes to fetch a bottle of red Burgundy. "Here, they've ordered this before."

"Just in case," he says, "let me have the names and addresses of the others missing in action. I'll keep trying." He notes down the details she gives him.

Back in his room, he Googles riding schools in Thornbury. Cotswold Event Centre, that must be where she works, he hopes. He notes the location. Just fifteen minutes from Dursley. If he's lucky it will save him from having to go Scottish dancing again and hoping Charlotte turns up. Not that he hadn't enjoyed the dancing. Quite enjoyed. But it's not his thing, not his crowd.

****

Even before he's opened the gate he can hear an amplified bass guitar throbbing the house. He knocks loudly but no-one answers, so he waits for a pause in the guitar throb, then knocks loudly again. The guitarist might have cans on. But this time, the door is opened, by a head of long, wild blonde hair sitting on top of a twenty-something man in an Atomic Rooster T-shirt and blue jeans. "Yeah?"

"You Kip Rawsthorne?"

"Yeah."

Charley hands him the bottle of Burgundy. "With compliments from Elira. You know? Elira?"

"Oh yeah. The dealer lady, right?"

"Right. Have you got a minute? I just want to ask you

something."

"Ask away, man." Rawsthorne doesn't invite him in.

"She's wondering why you've stopped buying from her lately."

"What?" He looks at the label. "Stopped buying Côtes de Nuits, you mean?"

"No, the other stuff you used to buy from her."

"Oh, right, the blow, you mean?"

"Yes."

A barefooted girl in a floral smock appears behind Rawsthorne. "¿Qué te pasa, calabaza?" she asks.

"Nada, nada," he tells her.

She puts her arm around his neck and whispers to him. He nods, gently nudges her, and she leaves, with a friendly little wave for Charley.

Charley says, "Yes, Elira has noticed…"

Rawsthorne interrupts. "Man, you know, you always look for the best deal."

"Better price, you mean?"

"That's right, better price. You nailed it. Better price."

"Same quality?"

"Ninety per cent Colombian. Don't want the street stuff."

"Could I ask you how much better the price is?"

"I don't really have the figures in my head, but this guy turned up, right here, and told me he knew what I was currently paying and he'd do it for 15 per cent off."

"Who was he, this guy? Someone you knew?"

"No, no, guy with a foreign accent, might've been Italian, or maybe Greek."

"And how did he know you could be interested? How did he

locate you?"

Rawsthorne shrugs. "I dunno. He just showed up, like you have, and he had a baggie, and he licks his finger and puts it in the baggie and says, 'Try that'. So I give it a try and it's good, the real thing, you know, and then he gives me this 15 per cent off offer, and I tell him, you're on. That's how it's been."

"Do you have any idea where he's coming from?"

Rawsthorne frowns. "Man, I don't like where you're going with this. Best if you move along, right?"

"Believe me, I'm no snitch. I'm just someone trying to help Elira with her trade. It's strictly business, you understand."

"Move along, please. You're making me nervous." And he shuts the door.

****

At the entrance to the riding school he is told that Charlotte has just finished a session with four children, and he'll probably find her over there in the stables, mucking out.

She is still in riding boots, but has put blue overalls on to wield a pitchfork at piles of mucky straw. Her back is to him as he approaches her. "Charlotte?"

When she turns, the pitchfork is pointing at him. "Hello." she says guardedly. There is a smear of muck on her cheek, which she wipes with the back of her hand.

"It's not the Peasants' Revolt. You don't need that to ward me off."

She lowers the pitchfork. It's only then, he can see, that she recognises him. "Charley, from the Scottish dancing?"

"Och aye."

"You told me about King Zog. What are you doing here? You want a riding lesson?" She gestures along the line of stalls, where he can see the heads of three horses.

"No, I've never sat on a horse, I'd be terrible. You might have to use the whip on me."

"You won't find a whip in this yard. How did you find me here?"

"You said you worked at a riding school around here, and there's only this one."

She throws the pitchfork at him, upright, so that he can catch the handle. "If you're not here to ride, then you've come to help me muck out."

"OK. Show me."

She does, and giggles as he tosses half a dozen forkfuls into a barrow. "I'll get you some overalls."

And she does, and for ten minutes, in his overalls, he works with her, and finds it enjoyable enough to half-mean it when he asks, "You're not looking for someone on this job?"

"No, 'fraid not. Why, you looking for a job?"

"I've already got one of those. That's what brought me up this way, and I thought I'd look in on you."

"You're delivering things for Elira."

"Well remembered. You went off without answering my question."

"What question?"

"Whether I could see you again."

"You're doing that now."

"But it would be more fun in a nice restaurant."

She takes her overalls off, and he follows suit. In her breeches and boots, carrying her helmet, she leads him out of the yard and into the car park, where he unlocks the BMW. "Nice car," she says, as he wanted her to say. "Look," she says, "I'm seeing someone."

"Sure, you're seeing me at this moment."

She is hesitating. "But he's just gone home to Trinidad, for a couple of months, so you could say I'm not solidly booked up on dinner dates right now."

"Great. Saturday evening?"

"Mmm. I can do that."

"I'll pick you up at 7.30. Where do I find you?"

"No, I'll meet you there. Where?"

"You know the Souk Kitchen, corner of Apsley Road?"

"I've never been there, but I know where it is."

"It's good. Middle Eastern food."

"Yummy."

"I'll book a table for 8pm." Pray god there's a table.

11

ELIRA TELLS HIM she has had her computer checked out for hacks. "It's clean, completely clean," they told me.

"Aren't you nervous they'll have seen what's in your order book?"

"I'm careful about that, don't worry. My clients are instructed to order kanevvluk. It's Eskimo for fine snow."

Charley grins. "Nice one."

"So we're none the wiser on that. And Kip Rawsthorne was no use?"

"All he was willing to tell me was that some chap, Italian or Greek he guessed, knocked at his door and offered him coke cheaper than he was paying. He couldn't say how the chap knew that he, Kip, was a potential mark."

"Or wouldn't say."

"No one, "Charley continues, "not even an Italian or a Greek, is going to knock on your door at random and ask, have you thought about double glazing, or might you be interested in buying some cocaine?"

"Someone has hijacked my client list."

"Right. Someone who could brief some recruit to pitch up and say, unfortunately Elira is no longer in a position to supply you, but she asked me to call in to help you out, and the good news is that I can offer you a better price."

"We're both thinking of the same name, aren't we?"

"It's got to be Wheen. All the time he was working for you he was keeping notes on the addresses. He got greedy."

"Greedy. And needy he is, that one. He wouldn't have done it while Jack was here. They were good friends. But after Jack died, he had a dart at me. Wanted to get into my bed. Urgh. I sent him packing."

"How would he be sourcing the stuff? Zamir wouldn't double-cross you, would he?"

"No. But Wheen did the Barking collection for me several times, and he could easily have made connections there outside Zamir's circle. New people are turning up all the time, according to Zamir, and they don't all play by his rules. Albanian rules. There's an influx of young ones from Kosovo, I told you about them."

"Yeah, I met one of them. Well, I don't know if he was Kosovar, but he had no respect for Zamir."

"What am I going to do?" Elira's hands are on her head.

"Do you want me to go and confront Wheen?"

"Would you? I'd be so grateful. You won't get a confession, of course, but it might put the wind up him."

"Perhaps I should take an AK47 with me."

"If you got enough out of him to nail him, you could try suggesting that you have a friend in the police."

"I do have, as it happens. We were at school together. But I don't think that's the way to go. Wheen would spill the beans on you, take you down with him."

"Yes, you're right. But still, if we knew that he's the one doing it, it would be a first step. I could see if Zamir was able to straighten things out at his end. He is influential. And it would be in his interest to stifle gang rivalry."

"I'll find Wheen for you. Tomorrow I've got two deliveries, yes?"

"One in Corsham, and one in Weston-super-Mare."

"We'll see how they go."

****

The deliveries go without any hitch. Wheen is playing his hand patiently.

When he gets back, Charley parks outside the county cricket ground in Bristol. He has checked that Gloucestershire are playing at home, against Lancashire. This might be the swiftest way to locate Wheen. If he is watching the match he'll be in the members' seats, but that should not be a problem. Charley knows Dave, the county groundsman. He's played both with him and against him in club games.

Dave is standing beside the sightscreen, watching the match. "Hullo, mate," he greets Charley. "What do you know?"

"Keep an eye on anything Dunlop sends out, at the moment. He had two winners and a second at the weekend."

"Dunlop." Dave nods. "Thanks. You seen this kid bowling from this end? Jason Grey. He's new this season. Watch how much he's bending it."

Charley watches, and sees the ball swing late, past the outside edge of the tailender facing. The Gloucestershire fielders shout encouragement. "Mmm," Charley agrees. "Handy."

"He started off with two grabbers up for the cherry. He's got good swag all right. It's what you need."

Charley looks at the scoreboard. "How're we doing? Lancs twenty ahead with eight down."

"See off this tail and get stuck in second dig, we could be in business. Won't be easy last day. It's wearing."

"You saw to that."

"I did. We just had to win the toss and get first knock."

"You saw to that too?"

"I wish. I used to have a double-headed penny, but it's gone awol."

"Dave, I need a favour. There's a bloke I want a word with and I think he might be in the members'. Could you take me through?"

At the end of the over, Dave jerks his head, Charley follows. Dave has a word with the security man guarding the gate, and they walk up the steps towards the pavilion. The members' seats are half-full. Wheen, in blazer and panama, is there, in a group of three. Charley walks along the row behind him, and taps Wheen's shoulder. Wheen turns abruptly, startled, then recognises him. "Ah, my dear chap," he says, not remembering Charley's name, "I wasn't expecting to see you here."

"I was hoping I'd find you. Could be a close match, this."

"Yes, yes, as long as we can get rid of this last couple cheaply."

"Something on which I'd like your advice. Not now. Can we meet some time?"

"One evening in the Old England?"

"I'd rather it was somewhere more private. It's a confidential matter."

"I'm not a practising solicitor any more, you know," Wheen says. One of the acquaintances sitting beside him chuckles to himself.

"No, it's not a legal thing," Charley tells him.

The chuckling acquaintance says, "So it's an illegal thing, then? Right up your street, Randolph, eh?"

All three of them find merriment in that. Charley doesn't. "Would it be possible for me to call on you at home?" he asks.

"When were you thinking?"

"Well, I expect you'll be watching here the next couple of days, so how about Friday?"

"Very well. I'll have the kettle on at tea-time, four-thirty, that suit you?"

"Fine. Four-thirty on Friday. Thank you. Can you tell me your address?"

"I'm in St Werburgh's, on Ladysmith Street, number 41."

"I'll see you there."

Shouts from the field signal the ninth wicket.

****

"He'll be slippery," Mike warns him, when Charley has told him about Wheen.

"I'll take my catch bag. Which reminds me, we haven't been fishing since, it must be last year."

They are sitting at a corner settle in the Coach & Horses. "Lawyers, they're the worst," Mike says. "You have to wonder, are they taught to be slippery, or are they born like that and hence doomed to wear silly wigs and talk pompous?"

"No, they're not the worst, politicians are." Charley puts on a posh voice: "The right honourable lady's point is well taken. What is going on that they have to act like it's still 1790? Is it that by speaking as though they were in some old play they can always pretend they don't really mean what they're saying, they're just reciting someone's script, it's not for real?"

"I don't agree. At least you don't hear MPs using Latin when there are perfectly normal English words for it. Caveat emptor! And all it means is, be a canny shopper."

"I think it means more than that."

"Oh yeah?"

"Something to do with who carries the can when your new kettle doesn't work."

"I defer to m'learned friend," Mike says, gripping the lapels his bomber jacket hasn't got.

"Or when the hamburger you just ate gives you the runs."

"That can't happen. Stick to the real world."

"Look," Charley says, pointing at the wide window. "Look at those – geese, are they? – up there. How do they decide who's at the front point of the V? Do they have a vote on it? Is it some bully-boy goose who thrusts himself in there? No, they are a community, with a natural understanding of who is best equipped to do the job of leading them. Do you suppose that number six right side goose is there because he's figured that it will position him better than number seven to catch two worms and number seven will have to make do with one? No. He knows by instinct, and so does number seven, that it all works out best for everyone if they go into that formation. They don't fly around tweeting like it's 1790 or singing in Latin to keep the lower-class geese in their place. They just know what's best for all, and that's all that matters."

Mike is shaking his head. "If Charles Darwin came in here now and sat down to have a pint with us, he wouldn't be agreeing with you. When people talk about survival of the fittest, they're looking at who's fittest. But the really important word is survival. I'm going to survive better than you if I eat two worms and you only get one. So bugger community. I want to keep my genes in play, that's what's driving me. And driving those geese. I could swallow another pint. How about you?"

"You're buying?"

"It's my turn, innit?"

"It is. But your survival prospects are better if you've got ten quid in your pocket and I've only got five."

"You know, Charley, I sometimes wonder how it is that we've remained best mates all these years when we can hardly find anything we agree about."

"If Karl Marx came in now to join us and Darwin on this settle he'd be telling you it's the dialectical principle. I make a case, you contradict it, and somewhere in the middle we find something we can both live with."

"And neither of us really accepts it."

"No, but we both make the best of it."

While Mike is buying the pints, Charley goes on thinking. What Wheen, and people like Wheen, the many people like him, are clinging desperately to is fear. They are frightened not so much of having only one worm, nor even of losing that one worm, but most of all frightened of seeing in the mirror someone who is not entitled to two worms.

12

IN THE PARKING bay outside Wheen's house is a Rover. Charley feels the bonnet. It is warm.

Wheen shows him into his sitting room. It is like a film set. On the walls, which are lined with red embossed wallpaper, are mounted trophy heads: rhino, stag, snarling lioness, ibex. Charley restrains himself from fingering them to check if they are real. Above an ornate sideboard are two cases of pinned butterflies. Fish swim in a two-yard long tank among weeds and shells. The floor is covered by several rugs, Persian in style. A glass-fronted bookcase appears to contain nothing but a complete set of Wisden starting with the 1864 edition. On top of the bookcase sit five silver trophies, two of them surmounted by golfing figures. The sofa and two armchairs are upholstered in silver leather. Wheen is dressed in a red-and-gold Chinese dressing-gown, with a yellow cravat, and brown suede slippers. When he motions Charley to sit down, it is as though the entire scene has been designed for this moment, and Charley has the first line to speak but he can't remember it. He just stares around him.

Wheen asks, "Do you like Earl Grey?"

"Yes. Thank you."

Wheen exits and reappears stage right with two cups in saucers, which he places on the brass top of a trestle table. "Sugar?"

"No, thank you."

"Not milk, right?"

"Right."

He fetches the teapot and fills the cups. "My wife is away, visiting her sister, so I have to be mother. Now, you said you have a confidential matter to discuss."

"I'm here on behalf of Elira." No director shouts from the stalls to correct his intonation, so he presses on. "She is anxious. She is losing some of her regular clients."

Well," Wheen shrugs, "people do die off, you know. Especially when they're using what Elira sells them."

"They're not dying. Not all of them, at any rate. I've met some who admit they have been buying from someone else."

"More cheaply, one might guess."

"Maybe. The question is, how has this new supplier got hold of their names and addresses?"

"Oh my. No wonder the dear lady is feeling anxious. It sounds to me as though someone must have hacked into her computer."

"No, she's had it checked. It's clean."

"Then you must have been followed. That's why she's always changing the number plates, to avert that risk. And to avert the police, of course. They're always on the lookout for people in your business. The riskiest trip is collecting from that estate in Barking."

"Yes, I've done that trip."

"Have you? I'm not surprised. She never liked doing that trip herself. The police know it's a hot spot for the trade. And the gangs there, the feuding gangs, with their knives and AK47s. And the 'Ndrangheta, you know? They're running the ships. Did you see any of that?"

"A little."

"Watch out for yourself in Barking, Charley. I never felt at ease when I went there for her. It will be some group from Barking who have cottoned on to Elira's trade. They won't try cornering all of it at once. That's not their way, the Albanians. It'll be catchee monkey time, slowly, slowly, so as not to draw attention. They prefer the stealthy approach, rather than violence, particularly the older, calmer heads. Negotiation if possible. They might get round to negotiating with her. She is half-Albanian herself, after all. They might continue supplying her, for the social contacts she's got and they'd find difficult to deal with. And they'd be happy to let her keep her trade in caviar and whatnot."

"That's not going to keep her in the style she's accustomed to."

Wheen shrugged again. "We all have to change our customs sometimes, you know? The Albanians, as far as I understand it, aim to take over the country region by region, slowly, long term, cutting out the middle men when they can. They might meet their match in the north-west, because the port of Liverpool has its own gang structures. But it all depends on who's behind it. If it's a rival gang to the people she knows, or, worse, if it's people from Naples, they might not be patient."

"Is that why you stopped working for her?"

"No, it was because of the drink/drive charge I was stupid enough to incur. I told you."

"What you told me doesn't always add up."

"Really? For example?"

"Well, for one thing, you didn't tell me what it really was I'd be delivering."

"Oh, Charley, come on... It wasn't going to take long for you to rumble."

"You took it for granted that I'd have no moral objection."

"And do you have?"

"As it happens, no. And there's the risk."

"Risk?"

"The gangs you were describing. And the police."

"I formed a judgment about you. Was I wrong?"

"You formed a judgment in the time it took me to unscrew a nut?"

"I did. I'm a solicitor, remember. I'm trained to judge people."

"Judges judge."

"So solicitors merely solicit?"

Wheen wants him to laugh. Charley doesn't laugh.

"Let's get back to what you've come about," Wheen says. "Can you tell me who's gone missing on the client list? I became good friends with some of the clients. I might be able to shed some light."

Charley brings out the list Elira had given him when he was deciding where to make enquiries. "Totnes, name of Duxford. Burnham-on-Sea, people called Hall. Bedminster, a woman with a German name – Rottweiler, is it?"

"Rottensteiner. Antje Rottensteiner, lovely woman."

"And in Devizes, John Smith, he calls himself."

"Yes, yes, I remember them all. It's a shame they've dropped off the list, some of them were charming. Antje in Bedminster, she always treated me to a nip of vodka. The Duxfords, they're very hospitable people. The chap in Devizes, I used to ask him his real name, strictly in confidence, but he would insist it was John Smith. The musician in Dursley, I could always hear him playing before the door opened. The only one I didn't much like was Mr Hall in Burnham. No conversation at all. But he was a regular order, and that's what you're looking for."

Breathe carefully. At last. Wheen had played a straight bat till now, but in his need to parade his bonhomie he had lost concentration. "I didn't mention the musician in Dursley," Charley says.

Wheen visibly stiffens.

"Kip Rawsthorne he's called."

"Yes, yes, I remember," Wheen answers.

"But how did you know he's gone awol too?"

"I — I didn't know, but he's the sort who might."

Charley says, "We knew it must be you. You're got all her clients stored in your head. You've been drip-feeding them to someone else, or maybe yourself, recruiting a front man. How could you do it, Randolph? Jack and Elira were your friends."

Wheen is silent. He looks as though he might be about to cry. Then he speaks. "You don't understand."

"I don't. That's why I asked the question."

"Jack was my friend, but Elira never has been. She's cold to me."

"That's as may be, but she's the widow of your friend."

"You don't understand."

"So you said."

"Did one of the clients blab about me?"

"That wasn't necessary."

"It wasn't my idea. I've been put under intolerable pressure. I have to take pills to get any sleep. There's someone else, you don't know him. He put me up to it."

"And you didn't argue?"

"I couldn't. He gave me no choice."

"If he had, what would the 'or' have been?"

"He'd have had me killed."

Charley closes his eyes and goes for it. "Like he did Jack?"

Wheen's mouth opens. He isn't breathing. Then, weakly, he says, "How did you know that?"

"Call it a lucky shot."

Wheen collects himself. This is not the play he'd thought he was in. He speaks more slowly, and intently. "He knew what Jack was up to. The firm had not been doing well, that's why Jack had diversified into cocaine, with Elira's connections, because our pay was pretty lousy. The man had even bought cocaine from him. And he likewise wanted more income, so he thought he'd get a bit of what he could see Jack and Elira were making. This was before I started doing the deliveries for them. She used to deliver then."

"This firm that wasn't doing well, this would be the law firm where you and Jack worked together."

"Yes. When Jack refused to cut the man in, he got Jack sacked. Fitted him up."

For the first time in months, Charley feels he's ahead of the game. Wheen hadn't realised how far into the quicksand he was stumbling. Charley is thinking quickly. "What Elira told me was that the man did his best to talk the senior partner out of it, out of striking Jack off."

"Oh yes, that's what he told Elira. But I was there. I saw what was going on."

"Having sacked him, why did he need to have Jack offed?"

"To clear him out of the way, that's all. So that he could move in and take over the business. An acquisition. It was, first get him out of our offices, to keep everything at arm's length, avoid any risk of tainting the good name of the firm, then see him killed. And the sacking would look like probable cause of the heart attack. But he'd reckoned without Elira."

"She's nobody's pushover."

"She wasn't having it, him moving in on the business. So his next move was that I, since I was coming up to retirement, I offer to do the deliveries for her, as an old friend, even though we've never really hit it off, but he wasn't to know that. She'd need someone now for deliveries. And I'd start passing on her client list to him. Gradually, to start with, so as not to alert her."

"How would he source the coke?"

"Me again. After a few months of delivering and collecting, I was able to give him a couple of names in Barking. People I'd met on my trips there, and had gathered wanted to muscle in on what Zamir's lot were supplying. People who were fairly new on the scene, a Kosovar, one of them, and an Italian from Naples. It's clannish, that place. No love lost. Look at the knifings you read about. And there are guns. The Albanians have preferred to keep the peace, because that's best for business, but when new people come in they don't want to follow the rules, they want to seize the throne."

"The hit on Jack, how did he fix that? It was put down as a heart attack."

"It was a heart attack. He fixed it himself. He's got an oleander in his garden. He rang Jack to have a round of golf with him at the club where they played, soon after the sacking. No hard feelings, that kind of schmoozing. And he bought a round before they teed off, and dosed Jack's pint with oleander. 'From my own garden,' he swanked to me. To scare me. It worked, as you can see. He's a very clever and dangerous man. Before he came to Bristol he was in Scotland, and I think was working for some branch of MI5 or MI6. That's where he would have picked up some of his tricks. James Bond stuff, isn't it? So poor old Jack collapsed vomiting on the fourth fairway, and they got him to hospital but it was no good."

"Wouldn't there have been a post-mortem?"

"Oh, there was, but they just wrote down heart attack. If they took a blood test they wouldn't have been looking for anything like oleander. There was no cause for suspicion. They're used to collecting people of Jack's age from the golf course."

"What you haven't mentioned is that you were there, at the golf course."

"We were playing a threesome, yes."

"But you didn't know what – you haven't told me his name – what the oleander man was planning to do?"

"Of course I didn't know. Jack was my friend."

"What's his name?"

"I'm not telling you that."

"It won't be hard for me to find out."

"What are you going to do with what I have told you?"

"I'll have to tell Elira."

"And she'll tell Zamir, and there will be blood on the streets of East London."

"So it goes," Charley says.

"It does."

"You never thought of going to the police?"

"Would you, in my situation?"

"That's a different question. Tell me this, are you going to stop leaking the clients, now that we've confirmed what's been going down."

Wheen thought about it. "I would like, I would very much like to stop it all. But I've shown you the pressure I have been under. I don't know that I can stop it."

"It's an addictive drug, treachery, isn't it?"

"You don't understand. You've got to realise, I could be the next one for a post-mortem."

"I'll put flowers on your grave, promise."

"You can joke about it."

Charley sees that the mounted lioness is showing her teeth not in a snarl but a laugh. He stands up. "Sleep well," he says, and exits.

13

IF, CHARLEY IS thinking, we work on the wild assumption that Wheen is for once not lying, then the partner who Elira believes had intervened on Jack's behalf but, according to Wheen, actually framed Jack and then poisoned him was, Elira had said, the father of Charlotte, Gordon something, and at this moment Charley is sitting at a table in the Souk Kitchen waiting for Charlotte. You have to smile. Grimly, if you want.

He stands up to greet her and truthfully tells her that she is looking wonderful, "now that you've wiped the horse dung off your cheek." It is a warm evening and she is wearing a floaty linen trouser suit with a floral pattern. Charley is in his best dark blue shirt and chinos.

They share about six dishes of mezze and a bottle of Côtes du Rhône. "I keep thinking it's Saturday," he says.

"It is Saturday."

"I know, and I can't stop thinking about it because it's the day I'm seeing you."

It's the day, and of course he is wondering how it will end up and, in particular, where. He's done his best to tidy up his bedsit, a short walk from here, but he's never been able to forget the girl who, entering his room for the first time, fanned her face with a hand and asked, "What do you do in here, breed owls?" There is a chance that Charlotte, used to mucking out stables, will not think this much worse, but she is also used to living in her parents' house and her father is a man who stands up tall for the national anthem and, though she protested that she is not a Daddy's girl, she will have domestic standards. He can only hope that the shelves (planks on bricks) of books might lend his room an air of Bohemian curiosity to redeem the squalor of the everyday. Baudelaire would not have had lace antimacassars in his room.

"These fried aubergines are delicious," she is saying, "fried to a crisp. Have you tried one?"

He tries one and agrees with her. "Do you cook?" he asks.

"Oh yes, I love cooking. After I left school I had a job for a few months in Keith Floyd's restaurant in Chandos Road. Officially I was a waitress, but I spent as much time as I could helping Jean-Claude in the kitchen. He taught me so much. How about you? Do you cook for yourself?"

"Not what you'd call cooking."

"What would you call it?"

"Sustenance."

"Beans on toast?"

"When I feel like splashing out."

"When you've won at the races."

"I know you don't approve of racing. I've already given you my defence of it."

"Yes, and you make a good argument."

"Thank you, m'lud. Your father's a lawyer, isn't he?"

"He is. How did you know?"

"Elira told me."

"You've been talking about me with Elira?"

"Only in passing. She mentioned your father when she was

telling me about her late husband. He worked with your father, didn't he?"

"He did. It was my father who got him and Elira into Scottish dancing."

"And now she's trying to get me into it. They're always short of men, she says."

"They are."

"Did you know Jack, her husband?"

"I'd meet him at the dancing, but we never had a proper conversation."

What he would like to ask her next is whether she believes her father could have poisoned Jack. Instead, he says, "Elira told me your father did his best to intervene when Jack was struck off as a solicitor."

"Was he? I never heard about that. All I knew was that he had dropped dead playing golf with my Dad. Awful. Is Elira still missing him?"

"I think so. She doesn't talk a lot about him. I haven't asked her what he'd allegedly done to deserve being struck off."

"Don't. It would just be another wound. Why do you want to know?"

"Call me Mr Nosey."

"I will. What I'd like to know is what they put into this excellent hummus. I must ask them. I could be cheeky and see if they'd let me look around their kitchen, like I used to at Floyd's. Jean-Claude, he was really old school. Once, I made the mistake of telling him how much I'd enjoyed reading about the 1968 riots in Paris, and there was this thick forefinger being wagged in my face, like a small tree trunk, and he growled, Les évènements, tout ça, c'est de la connerie. How's your French?"

"What's French for non-existent?"

"He was saying, the protests, they were all bullshit."

"Well, I can't see they changed much. Like the Black Panthers. Nothing changes. Though Heraclitus says…"

"You're getting back at me for my bit of French."

"Heraclitus says, No man steps into the same river twice."

"How's your Greek?"

"Oh leave it out. Let's get back to Jack. Is there anyone at your Dad's firm you could ask about it?"

"About Jack being struck off, you mean?"

"Yes. I don't imagine you could ask your Dad, but are you matey with one of the secretaries, say?"

"If you insist, Mr Nosey. There's Joanna, she might know something. If I see her I'll try to remember."

""It's just so that I don't inadvertently say something that would upset Elira."

"She's your boss. Are you on such close terms with your boss that you need to be so protective?"

"Now it's you being Ms Nosey. There is nothing going on between her and me. It's just that she does like to talk. A lot. She's lonely. She's only got her daughter. So I suppose I do feel a bit protective. There are decent veins even in a wretch like me."

"A man with feelings for an older woman. It's a small step for feminism, I guess."

"I'm all for it. I told you, I'd give a shout for communism if someone would give it a run. Or let's call it communitarianism, to take the stink of Stalin away."

"I'll never trust in any kind of ism. They all get corrupted."

"So what do you believe in?"

"Horses. People. Well, some people. Good food. Snooker."

"Snooker?!"

"Yes. Do you fancy a frame after this?"

"Where, on The Triangle?"

"No, we've got a table at home."

"You're inviting me to go home with you? What'll your parents think?"

"They're in Scotland for a week."

****

She drives them in her green Mazda 2 to the detached mock-Tudor house in Stoke Bishop. The best break Charley can achieve is 12. She runs up an eight-ball 25 in the first frame and a 41, including three blacks, in the next. She has a smooth cueing arm, a sensitive touch with the tip. Watching her play, he finds it sexy, albeit he is haplessly outclassed. After two frames he raises his glass to her and enjoys the armagnac she has poured. "Slim lady, you shoot a mean game," he says, from a deep leather armchair.

"It helps that I've grown up with a table in the house," she replies.

"And you didn't even hustle me."

"What do you mean, hustle?"

"Let me win a frame, then put money on it."

She sits down on his lap, her glass carefully poised, and asks, "Would you play an immoral trick like that?"

"Morality can be contingent, don't you think? It might depend upon whether I liked my opponent."

"I don't like the sound of that, contingent morality. It's not what I was taught in philosophy."

"Your school had philosophy classes?"

"No, that was at Oxford. But I dropped out after two terms. Came back here."

"Why?"

"I realised I'm not academic. I could do the essays all right, and the tutorials, it wasn't that I was no good. Just, it didn't suit me, that way of thinking. Too abstract."

He puts his arm around her and kisses her cheek, near her mouth, gently. "I couldn't hustle you," he says. "I like my opponent."

She kisses him back, on the lips, and continues, "I was having a good time socially. That's where I met Vivian, my boyfriend."

Nicely done, Charley thinks. A cuddle and a kiss, okay, but remember I've got a boyfriend. She's drawn a line, sketched in the contingency. He replies, "He's in Trinidad, you said?" Just testing.

"Yes. He's gone to see his parents. His father's not well."

"Are they a black family?"

"Viv is brown, gorgeous brown, like a chestnut. Not like us, who call ourselves white, when really we're patchy pink and beige. He's still the colour that came out of Africa a million years ago, but here, in the north, we've become – well, the word for it is 'etiolated', you know?"

"Tell me."

"It means drained of colour, faded. Like a flower in the cellar. I think that's what's going on when people are trying to get a tan. Yearning for ancestral roots, yes?"

Charley scratches an earlobe with his spare hand. "It's a pretty theory," he says.

"Don't be so damn mealy-mouthed. It's not a theory, it's an observation. Shall we continue this argument in bed?" She stands up, holding his hand.

"I didn't know we were having an argument," he says.

"I did."

She'd zapped him at snooker and now he finds himself lengths behind her in this game, too, struggling to make up the ground. He is meek as he follows her upstairs to her bedroom, where she undresses and gets between the sheets, and he does likewise. He strokes the sides of her body, which she enjoys, he kisses her breasts. Holding hers, he likes his own body. As far as he can tell (a man can't be sure) their joy is in synch.

Their heads are on the pillows, face to face. He strokes her cheek, and says, "You know, in old Japan, when a samurai was taken by surprise he was permitted to kill the surprising one."

"Don't tell me you're surprised. That evening when we met, at the dancing, I could see where you were heading – here."

"I can be surprised that I got here. You left without even saying goodnight."

"I wanted time to think it over."

"And what was your thinking?"

"I was thinking you're not brutish looking, and you make me laugh, and you seemed to have a bit going on in there" – she taps his skull – "but what decided me was when you took the trouble to track me down at the stables."

"You might have put me down as a stalker."

"You haven't got the mad eyes to be a stalker. You're a talker, not a stalker. I like your eyes."

"If I start telling you what I like in you we'll be here all night."

"We will be here all night."

Charley is checked. "Where do I start?"

"Unless you've got to go and deliver something for Elira?" she continues.

"Not till Monday. I could happily lie here all night and all day tomorrow, if you like. Very happily."

"I'm giving riding lessons at eleven."

"Will your boyfriend monster me if he finds out?"

"God, no. We're not like that. It's the age of the pill, thank god."

"I should have checked that out with you, sorry."

"You should have, but I can take care of myself. I'm no believer in monogamy. That's your generation's thing."

"My generation? I'm only old enough to be your big brother."

"But you've got older ways about you, haven't you?"

"You're talking about class, not generation."

She thinks for a moment, then says, "You're right. But the point I was making is that for many generations, forever probably, men have always had flings, felt it was their right, why has there been a different standard for women?"

"Not always. Not everywhere. Not in France, for example. Not here in the 18th century. Sorry about that, I've just been reading about duchesses at that time. Georgiana Cavendish, you know? What a woman. Ancestor of Princess Di."

"I surprised you because you had me down as an English rose. Just a little bit of a sexist aren't you, Charley?"

He waves his hand dismissively. "You surprised me because you take my breath away. In many ways. I've never known anyone as enlightened as you. No wonder you got into Oxford."

"And no wonder I dropped out."

"Does your boyfriend have the same views as you have about monogamy?"

"Sure. He might be in bed with some Trinidadian girl right now. We should all greet our pleasures as they present themselves. Life is short."

"As the Romans said, only it would impress you more if I could quote it in Latin. Do you tell each other?"

"We don't have secrets, but we're not nosey, either, or gabby. We're straight with each other. That's the way to make it last."

"So it's just this once for you and me?"

"I didn't say that. But one day I want to marry him, not you."

"Not that I've proposed to you, but why?"

"He's training to be a vet. He's great with horses. That's my life."

"There's nothing of a romantic in you, is there?"

"Oh no. I don't want to wind up like my mother, used up."

****

In the morning she wakes him up with a cup of coffee. "It's a beautiful day outside," she says. "Let's have a walk round the garden. It's my father's pride."

The garden is a big, circular lawn, immaculately mown. Flower beds run all around the perimeter, and behind them is an unbroken circle of cypresses, yews, a sycamore, holly, and a few smaller fruit trees, creating a perfectly enclosed haven. Nothing of the small, aligned rectangles among which Charley had grown up in Bedminster. "No wonder your father's proud of it."

"He makes the executive decisions. My mother does most of the work."

"You could play snooker on a lawn like this."

"We do have a croquet set somewhere. My brother and I used to play."

"You hadn't mentioned a brother. Does he still live here?"

"No, he's in Edinburgh, with an insurance company. Wife and two small kids. That's where my parents are this week."

"Most of the gardening work I get is on allotments, so I'm not very clued-up about flowers. Tell me, is there an oleander here somewhere?"

"Yes." She leads him across the lawn, and he bends over to smell the red petals. "Careful," she warns him, "don't let it touch you, it will give you a rash. How on earth did you guess we'd have an oleander?"

"I haven't got to where I am without some social savoir-faire."

"Exactly where is it you have got to, with delivering and decorating and gardening?

"I've got here, with you. What more could a man want?"

"Thank you, but I think you've done enough gallantry and flattering for now. I could probably handle a bit more of it from time to time."

"I'd like to hope there will be time to time."

"We need each other's mobile numbers." She brings out a ballpoint. "Give me your hand." She writes her number on the back of his hand, passes the pen to him and holds out her hand.

As he writes his number on her, he says, "By the way, I met a chap who I think used to work with your father. Randolph Wheen?"

She makes a face. "Yes. Creepy. Is he a pal of yours?"

"No, just an acquaintance, through work. Did he ever come here to see your Dad?"

"Now and then he did. Not regularly, thank god. I'd always avoid catching his eye. Now, I've got to get ready for work. I'll give you a lift over to the Blackboy."

"Thanks, but no need. It's a lovely day for a walk across The Downs."

"Give me a kiss goodbye." He puts his arms around her, and she grins at him. "You know how to kiss me, don't you? You just put your lips together and think of Lauren Bacall."

Walking across Clifton Down, past hawthorn bushes and clumps of people, students, office workers, he is deeply contented, yet sad. Feeling a bit out of date, he realises. But limerence, he reminds himself. That word. It could never have lasted.

14

HIS DELIVERIES ON Monday are all in Bristol, two in Easton and one in Bedminster, the street next to where he had grown up, so he has plenty of time to tell Elira about his meeting with Wheen, He must not mention Wheen's allegation that Charlotte's father had poisoned Jack. It could wreck her. Or bring the fuzz sniffing. Or kanun, that word for a blood feud she had taught him. And the bookies would go 4/6 it was a lie. Disentangling the truths in what Wheen tells you is harder than panning for fruit in sticky jam. Wheen had visited the house in Stoke Bishop, so he could have spotted the oleander for himself. It was a story that buttressed the pressure he said was on him. It all fitted together, the law firm needing more income, the framing of Jack and striking him off, the planting of Wheen as an informant, all fitted like a magician's set of boxes, and hey presto, nothing there, how did he do that?

But the meeting had achieved its immediate purpose. He can assure Elira that Wheen is the leak, and will go on leaking.

She nods. "It had to be him. The bastard."

"He was coming on with his self-congratulatory whiffle about what good friends of his the clients are, but he missed a step, added in Rawsthorne in Dursley, and I hadn't mentioned that one. At that point he changed tack, told me how murderous the pressure on him is, so it's not his fault, is it?"

"Pressure from whom?"

"Some cock and bull story again, but it looks as though he's working for a rival gang in Barking."

"Zamir needs to know about this. He might be able to sort it at his end. They're undercutting me, I'll have to undercut them, what else can I do? It's a race to the bottom, no good for anyone. That bastard. I'm amazed he let you into his house. Has he still got all those ghastly animal heads stuck up?"

Hold on, Charley is thinking. She'd been very vague about where Wheen lived, now it turns out she knows the inside of his house. He lets it pass. That's not in his casebook. "Yes," he replies. "He must have some fantasy life about being a big game hunter. Probably Ernest Hemingway's best mate. I'm guessing why he let me visit him is because if he hadn't it would have looked as though he'd got something to cover up."

"Which he had, in spades."

"Just as he told you he couldn't go on delivering for you because of a drink/drive charge, but the bonnet of his car outside his front door was warm when I felt it. It can't have been his wife had been out in it, She was away, visiting her sister."

"She's been away for at least ten years."

"Very close sisters they must be. So the drink/drive story was made up to cover his switch of loyalties. And recruiting me was another smokescreen, to look like he cared about quitting. Anyone would do. I turned up at the right moment for him."

"I'm glad you did, Charley. Things had got tense between him and me. I'd been running a little business of my own in the luxury goods, but when Jack lost his job we talked about it and decided to add cocaine to the shopping list because we needed income. I'd got the connection to Zamir. He's family. And I don't know if Jack told him about it, but Wheen, who'd got the chop at the same time, wanted in on our trade. For the time being he was just delivering. After Jack died, he thought, right, I'll take his place. But I needed the income, with Roze's school fees and everything else, so I kept him to delivering. And it wasn't just the business but soon, as I told you, he had his piggy eye on my bed, too. Talk about mergers and acquisitions. He'd made eyes at me even when Jack was still here. When I said No! to all of that, things cooled fast. So for him there's an element of sweet revenge in this."

"Talk to Zamir. Would you like me to go with you?"

"No, no. It's family. We'll be talking in Albanian."

He walks home via St Michael's Hill. He always enjoys the view across the old city, but his immediate purpose is to call in at Tim's bookshop on Park Row. It is a three-storey early Victorian building. Tim lives in the basement. The upper floors are a warren of second-hand books in which the borderlines between sections would provoke bloody frontier battles, but Tim can always locate at once any title you request or point you to a row of spines on the subject you nominate. He has a stand devoted to the work of local authors. If you want a newly published book he will get it in for you the same week. On the ground floor there is a long refectory table, with bentwood chairs. He allows people to sit there for hours, reading, talking to each other or to him, playing chess. Only chess is allowed, because he has a deep respect for the game. Fresh coffee is on the go, at 50p a mug. You can, if you wish, take a book home and return it with no charge, though he does let customers know that he would appreciate a 50p donation and most of them are happy to oblige. On the wall is a notice: Thieves will not be prosecuted. His theory, he says, is obvious: "treat people generously and they will be honest. Yes, of course I suffer some pilfering, and a few readers who have no intention to buy anything. I believe they cost me less than I gain from the support of the decent majority, and the unquantifiable benefit I enjoy from spending my days in a good ambiance." How he balances his accounts and pays his bills is a mystery concealed in the basement. Charley's appetite for reading, and following through threads of interest from one book to another, have been nurtured for years in this shop. He owes Tim, and his commercial philosophy, a great deal.

They sit at the table with mugs of coffee. "How're you doing?" Tim asks.

"Oi vey," Charley shrugs. "Good Yiddish?"

"You might get by in Bucharest."

"I'm struggling to get by in Bristol. It's not about money, it's that I've got myself involved in a situation, I can't give you names or details, gotta protect the innocent, but that's the trouble, I don't know who the innocent are. I won't say I'm clueless, I've got too many clues, and they contradict each other. Because people tell lies. I've dealt with a few villains in my time but they've mostly been honest villains. These people now, middle-class types most of them, what they say is calculated to get you where they want you, no more than that. Telling you the truth would be a waste of speech for them. I just don't know who to trust."

"What is it you want from them?"

"There's a woman I'm doing some work for and her business is under threat from rivals, and she's treated me decently so I feel some commitment to her. Only that, I'm not involved with her, nothing like that. I feel a bit sorry for her, and well pissed-off with what I know about the people she's up against. They don't have a scruple between them. Plus there's quite a big back story there of which I've gathered only fragments. I'm bewildered every day. So I suppose the best answer to your question is, what I want is to understand it all."

"You won't. When we've finished our coffees, go upstairs to the science section and find a book by Fritjof Capra called The Turning Point. In it you'll read about the Uncertainty Principle in quantum mechanics. You don't then have to spend the next ten years trying to understand quantum theory, and if you did you'd fail, because one of the great theoretical physicists, Richard Feynman, said that anyone who says they understand quantum theory has proved just one thing, that they don't understand it. No one can. Yet it stands up in every experiment. But what Capra will offer you is a way of living with not understanding. That's what you need, Charley."

"What I need is not understanding, you're telling me?"

"No. You haven't followed me. What you need is peace of mind. Live with the questions. Stand back from them and see yourself as someone grappling with them, not someone frustrated by a lack of answers. Capra has a beautiful phrase for it. When a physicist is observing the behaviour of subatomic particles it is impossible for him, or her, to be certain of, at the same time, the position and the momentum of any one particle. That's the Uncertainty Principle, and Capra sums it up as: 'there are no dancers, there is only the dance.' You get me?"

"I get you. I think. I'm not certain."

"Perfect. Now you can relax a bit. Don't stop asking the questions, if you want to give this woman help. But accept that what matters is the asking, the journey, not the destination. If you come in here next week and tell me you've nailed the answer, the one thing I'll know is that you haven't. No one's life is a detective novel with a pat ending."

Charley takes out a pound coin. "Tim, when I put this in your box for the coffees it will feel as though I'm making my Sunday contribution in the plate."

"Bless you, my son, and rejoice in the Lord, or whatever you have instead of God."

"I'm not certain."

"There is only the dance."

Charley leaves the shop with Capra's book. and will read it. But not yet. First, there is the question of the 4.40 at Warwick.

****

Elira goes to London for two days, and Charley catches up with painting two rooms for Mrs Symes in Dunkerry Road, an old family friend and neighbour. "I was wondering if you'd forgotten about it," she says.

"I don't forget. Sorry, m'dear. They needed me at a crisis meeting in Downing Street."

"Go on with you. What was the crisis, what colour they want the parlour painted?"

"You've got it. You must have a hot line to the Cabinet Secretary."

"Oh, there's not much gets past me. Did you enjoy your meal at the Souk Kitchen?"

He stares at her. "How on earth – "

Chuckles. "I've been saving that one for when I wanted to land it."

"Hold on. Your daughter, she's a cook, right?"

"Right. It's not what you know, it's where you've got your spies. She didn't want to interrupt your chat-up. Nice girl, the one you were with, is she?"

"She's lovely. I had a great evening. And the cooking there is something."

"Glad to hear it. I'll tell her what you said next time she calls in."

"She's not living at home any more, then?"

"Oh no. She got married last year, didn't you hear?"

"Living up the Blackboy, I lose touch with the real world down here."

"You not thinking of getting married?"

"I'd marry that girl your Brenda saw me with, but she's spoken for."

"That's a shame."

"Now come on, Mrs Symes, enough already with the marriage counselling. Are you quite sure about this shocking pink?"

"It's just what it needs, this room. Never gets any sunlight."

She goes to make a pot of tea and he goes on thinking about Charlotte. Pointless to wonder if she might change her mind about her bloke in Trinidad. He's seldom met a girl so certain about what she wants. He likes that. Splish splosh splish splosh, the paint goes on, smoothe it over with the brush flat, you know where you are, painting a wall, you've got fixed parameters. As they say.

He stops when the cup of tea arrives. Mrs Symes says, "It's a relief to me, seeing Brenda married off to a nice chap. Just a pity, my Harry would've been so proud to give her his arm up the aisle. It's my boy, Kenny, you remember him, is worrying me."

"What's the worry?"

"He won't tell me the truth, of course, but I'm pretty sure he's been messing around with drugs. There's a lot of it going on around here."

"It'll just be a phase he's going through."

She rolls her eyes. "Easy for you to say, Charley, but in the paper every day there's a story about some kid dying from an overdose."

"Is he working?"

"He's stacking shelves over in Asda."

"It's a big store. He'll work his way up there to some proper position, and he'll forget about drugs."

"I wish I could feel so confident about that. If Harry was still here he'd get him sorted. But I can't talk to him like a father would. Like your father, Ted, would have, if it was you. I wonder, could you perhaps have a word with him for me? He's known you since he was little. He'll listen to you. You don't mind me asking?"

"I'll give it a try for you, Mrs Symes."

"Bless you. I'd be so grateful."

Splish splosh splish splosh. Charley smiles to himself. Grimly.

15

ELIRA IS BACK from London. Zamir was sympathetic, she says, and will be doing what he can to locate those who are hijacking her clients, and to persuade them that co-existence, not invasive competition, is what has been working well for all concerned. But he is worried. New faces have been appearing. He'd instanced a group of brutal Italians from Foggia, who have been allied with the Calabrians with whom his Albanians have been co-operating for years, but may now be becoming rivals. And the gangs based in Liverpool, with Irish connections, bringing cocaine in through the container port, are extending their markets beyond the north-west, looking to corner all the trade outside London. It could well be them who are stealing Elira's clientele, and Zamir has no line of connection there. "I'd told him about what you'd got out of Randolph Wheen, and Zamir said our best hope is to squeeze the truth out of Wheen, who it is he's working with."

"I did try that, but he wouldn't squeal. He said, if he did he could be next for a post-mortem. Next after your husband, he meant."

"Was he suggesting Jack was killed?"

"I didn't want to tell you that. It must be upsetting for you, I'm sorry. But yes. He told me that Jack was poisoned, and – I might as well tell you the whole story – he said it was Gordon McFinn who did it, when they were playing golf together." Charley stops talking, while Elira stares unblinking at him. Then he adds, "Gordon McFinn who you go Scottish dancing with. But, Elira, you know that Wheen spews out lies. My own suspicion is that, if Jack was killed, it's at least as likely that it was Wheen himself who killed him. He was there that day, at the golf course. You told me."

Elira has closed her eyes. Charley stays silent. "The postmortem," she says eventually, "came up with nothing suspicious. Just a heart attack."

"Wheen says the poison was oleander, and they could have missed that. They should test for it."

"Oleander. I didn't know that was poisonous."

"Very poisonous, so I understand."

"He said Gordon... Why?"

"To get Jack out of the way so that he could muscle in on your trade."

She thinks for a while. Charley is relieved the story hasn't reduced her to tears. She says, "Not Gordon... It was Gordon who did his best to protect Jack when there was that trouble at the firm. No, Wheen is making that up to cover his own filthy arse. Gordon is a cold customer, but he's not a murderous one." She is shaking her head.

Charley prefers to change the subject. "As for what Zamir said, I doubt if the Liverpool lot are your problem. Wheen, when I was pressing him, said something about using connections he'd made in Barking with a new bunch coming in, and that there would be blood on the streets of East London if Zamir tried to intervene. He suggested Kosovars, but it sounds as if this new Italian lot could be in the frame."

"Zamir is looking into that. He has a plan, to arrange a high-level meeting with them and the Calabrians, and put it to them, as well as his own Albanians, that everyone will do better if they can co-operate."

"Good luck with that, Zamir."

"Well, it's worth a try. You know what they say about honour among thieves."

Charley grunts. "I know what they say."

"Charley, you must be wondering what kind of web you've got yourself entangled in here. I'm sorry, I only wanted you to help me with the deliveries, that's all. I'd just like you to know that I am very grateful to have you around to share my sorrows."

He nods in acknowledgment. "I've been in fixes before, don't worry."

****

He's been in fixes before, but this time it's next to impossible to read the form. A big field, plenty of fancied runners, and all the tipsters in disagreement. He starts to walk home. A walk is good for clearing his head, on a sunny day His telephone buzzes. "Charley?"

"Charlotte. Good to hear your voice."

"I've got something to tell you. Can we meet up soon?"

"I'm delivering the next couple of days, but evenings are okay."

"Not for me. I've got things to do with my mother."

"Saturday, then?"

"No, I'm eventing. Sunday afternoon?"

"Fine. Where? Another snooker match, get my revenge?"

"Can't do that here, now they're back from Scotland. Let's just go for a nice walk. I'll meet you by the Cabot Tower on Brandon

Hill, three o'clock?"

"I'll be there."

He'll be there, and will spend the next three days telling himself to stop fantasising that the plane from Trinidad could crash and, even if it did, could he imagine that a classy girl like Charlotte would ever want more than a fling with a delivery driver with a gambling habit? His father had taught him not to expect such things.

He stops off at Fred's shop, and as he had hoped Mike is in there, frowning at the 3.45 at Doncaster. "Charley, what have you heard?"

"I have heard that in this clan…"

"Please don't try singing. It's on your not-to-do list, remember."

"It cheers me up."

"And drains the cheer from anyone who hears you."

"I've been keeping an eye on Simcock. He started the week with a double at Salisbury."

"Simcock." Mike scans the paper. "He's got nothing going in this one."

Charley shrugs, and examines the runners. "It's fourteen furlongs. Try Johnston. He trains them to treat the winning post as the first stage."

"I've got nothing better, so I'll give it a go."

Johnston's horse finishes fourth. "It was running on at the finish," Charley observes.

"I'll keep it in mind for the Grand National."

"Mike, what do you know about quantum mechanics?"

"Where's it running?"

"It's not a horse, it's a branch of physics. I'm reading a book about it. It counsels us to accept living in a state of uncertainty. Permanently."

"You don't need counselling for that. It's common knowledge. Especially in here. It shouldn't be called a betting shop, it should have a big sign outside, The Emporium of Uncertainty."

"But the point is, accepting it. Look at them all, politicians, preachers, adverts, columnists, wellness gurus, they all come on as the one who knows. And they're phoneys, the lot of them. They're all trying to sell us certainty. When you splash out for some fancy car – "

"Chance would be a fine thing."

" – the only ads you'll ever read will be for the car you've just lumped on because you don't want to be told you could have bought something better, or cheaper. You want the certainty of not being a mug. They've got a name for that, the reduction of something or other."

"Cognitive dissonance," Mike suggests.

"How did you know that?"

"It's the only word for it. Or words."

"Just sometimes, Mike, you…" Charley shakes his head. "Anyway, whenever I hear some phoney trying to tell me what's what, definite, no room for doubt, I say to myself, 'On the other hand.' If I ever wrote a book, that's what I'd want to call it, The Other Hand."

"Good title. All you need now is thousands of good words to follow it."

Charley is walking home, then changes his mind, goes to the top of the hill and onto The Downs. There will be girls there in groups sunning themselves, girls with legs. Charlotte is still in his thoughts. When you meet someone you think might matter and you don't even try, you'll curl up and shrivel. He walks past a bunch of boys kicking a rugby ball around. Students, probably, from posh schools. Further on there is a group of eastern girls, from one of the local language schools they'll be. With a twinge of shame he can't help remembering that when he was a kid he and his mates, sniggering in doorways, believed that Japanese and Chinese women had transverse slits. It had been affirmed by Brian Talbot, the playground bully. Not only did you not argue with him, you respected his worldly wisdom. Charley's lot believed it, along with mounds of other junk thrown up by sexual apprehension. When they were all about eight, Brenda Dean used to let them look at her slit, but they never knew what to make of it. Brenda would exact payment, an apple or chocolate biscuit or something, for letting them look, so she already knew there was a transactional value in these matters. He doesn't remember that any girl ever wanted to look in a boy's pants. It's odd, he thinks, this looking business. It's the male invasion that is thrilling, the transgression of taboo. That is why virginity has always been prized, and any new lover is enhanced by a sense of conquest, a conquest of sense. A woman in her wholeness, wholly attended, is the prize a man learns to value, leaving behind in adolescence the thrill of looking, though many, not even James Joyce, don't get that far, as the sad rows of magazines on top shelves attest. Which reminds him that on his way home he must stop at the shop and buy a loaf of bread.

16

TWO DAYS LATER, as he leaves on his way to Bruton, he notices a silver Audi R8 pull out from where it was parked, opposite Elira's garage, and follow him down past the infirmary. It is still there, fifty yards behind, as he proceeds down the Wells Road. He drives calmly, in case it is the police on his tail. At Shepton Mallet he deliberately takes a long way around, through Castle Cary, and circling back up to his client's house in Bruton. The Audi follows, all the way. It carries on past after he has stopped, but he is sure it will not be the last he sees of it. Whoever it is must want him to know that he has been followed, otherwise they would have been more evasive, or chosen a more discreet car. The police would surely have stopped and inspected him. It must be Wheen's lot. But why? They don't need to sniff out the whereabouts of clients. Wheen will have given them all the addresses, including Elira's. The only conclusion he can reach is that it is a warning, a menacing gesture. We have our eye on you. He drives on to a second delivery, just outside Bradford-on-Avon, and doesn't see the Audi again, but he doesn't need to. They have made their point for now. It leaves him rattled, but angry too. Why can't they settle for their market share and leave ours to us, in peaceful co-existence?

He tells Elira about it, when he gets back. She nods, knowingly. She recognises this kind of intimidation. Her hope is in Zamir the Peacemaker, and she has news. Zamir has arranged the high-level meeting with the other contending parties. It will take place in a racecourse box at Royal Ascot. "He thinks something flashy like that will impress the others and give him the moral advantage."

Charley says, "Royal Ascot is the week after next. He'll do well to get a box at such short notice."

"He's already got it. One of his cousins had it booked for a family occasion, but Zamir has persuaded him that he needs to let us use it instead. Force majeure, as they say."

"Do they?"

"In Albanian they do. Charley, you know something about horse-racing, am I right?"

"You are right."

"Well, I know nothing, so I think you must accompany me to the meeting and tell me what bets I should make. I would have wanted you to come in any case, even if we were meeting in the Savoy Hotel. I need you there as my – let's say aide-de-camp."

"Everything sounds so decorous when you say it in French. Do you want me to pack protection of some sort?"

"What do you mean?"

"A weapon."

"Oh god no, it won't be like that, not at all. It will just be talking. Deal making. Reaching agreements."

He can't tell her, but the picture that had immediately come to mind was the mafia banquet in Some Like It Hot when a chap jumps out of the giant birthday cake with a tommy-gun and wipes out George Raft and his hoodlums and the Mussoliniesque head honcho says, "Sump'n in da cake didn't agree wid dem." But it won't be like that, not at all. And he's never been in a box at Royal Ascot and wasn't expecting to be, ever, and he does know something about horse-racing. Just wait till he tells Mike about it. No, hold on, he can't tell Mike, because Mike wouldn't be able to keep it to himself, he might as well post it up on the internet. Omertà is required. There's probably a word for that in French, or Albanian.

He asks Elira, "do I need to hire a morning suit and grey topper?"

"Not unless you want to cut a dash, or audition for My Fair Lady. We won't be in the royal enclosure. Just a suit and tie will do. And polish your shoes."

A pair of black shoes he's got, remember to buy some polish. As for a tie, he can't remember when he last wore one, but he's got a few at the back of the wardrobe, there's something stripey to do with a cricket club he once joined, that should pass muster. But a suit? Since he is only following her orders he doesn't mind asking Elira if by any chance her late husband was around his size and if she still has one of his solicitor suits that he might borrow.

She shrugs. "He was about your height, but a little fuller in build. Wait there." She comes back with two grey suits, one plain and one pin-striped, and points him toward the bathroom. "In there, try them on." When he reappears in the plain suit she says, "Mmm, yes, there's a bit to spare around the waist."

"I can take that in with a belt."

"All right. The jacket will cover up any gathers, as long as you keep it buttoned up. I think we can get away with it. Leave the suit here for now. I'll make sure it's nicely pressed and have it ready for you on the day."

****

On top of Brandon Hill on Sunday he makes a wide, sweeping gesture across the view of South Bristol and says, "That's me. That's where I come from."

"You're being very imperial," Charlotte tells him. "That's half the city you're laying claim to."

"All right, that bit there," he points. "The newer people like to call it Windmill Hill, and that bit over there the estate agents have branded as Southville, but, growing up, it was all Bedminster to me. Dockers and tobacco workers and in the old days coal miners, we all knew each other on the streets. Bemmies, we were. Not many left like that. The docks have gone, the tobacco's gone, the mines went years ago. My Dad worked in the docks when he was a young man. He told me about it, had his black book that you had to wave in the Pen to catch the eye of the gaffer who was handing out jobs for the day, if you were lucky, if you were one of his Blue Eyes. The Pen, that was like the cattle market where they all gathered in the morning. It's still there, you can see it, a little building on Prince Street, opposite the Arnolfini. Look at it now and you can't imagine how it used to contain five hundred men, all waving their little black books, hoping for a day's wages." He shakes his head. "And my Dad said the union, the TGWU, were useless at trying to get improved conditions. He'd snort if he heard the name of Ernie Bevin, who had founded the union. 'They make him Foreign Secretary,' he'd say, 'and when he started he was peddling soft drinks around the houses. Good morning, madam, would you care for some lemonade today, or can I interest you in my policy for dealing with the Soviet Union? Ernie Bevin, pah!' That was my Dad."

"He taught you some good values," Charlotte says. "What I believe in I had to teach myself."

"Oh yes. I owe him a lot. He belonged to that generation of Socialists that George Orwell mocked as bearded fruit-juice-drinkers and sandal-wearers. But what did Orwell know about it? He was an Etonian. One of the claret-drinkers and top-hat-wearers."

"Steady on, Charley. He outgrew all that, after Burma, and Spain."

"I know he did, I'm only saying it to stir you up."

"Do I need stirring up, with a view like this, right over to Mendip?" she asks.

"Argument is good, don't you think? It's a work-out for the brain."

"Oh, don't worry, I'll argue with you till the cows come home and go out again the next morning. That's what I was hoping for at Oxford, but I couldn't find much of it. Maybe it was my fault, I fell in with the wrong crowd."

Charley turns and gestures at the Cabot Tower behind them. "And this, I ask you. They stick this tower up in the 1890s to commemorate a man, an Italian man, who discovered North America – Columbus never did – and came back just pissed off that he hadn't found a way to China and Japan, which was all he was interested in. The spices of the Orient, the gems, that's what he was after. And at the time the people in Bristol would gladly have lynched him, because they'd already been going over there for the shoals of cod, off the coast of Newfoundland, teeming they were, and now bloody John Cabot had blown their cover and all the Portuguese and Spaniards would be at it, catching all the cod. But four hundred years later the merchants of Bristol declare he's such a great explorer he deserves a tower, with a light on top of it winking out Bristol in morse code. And at the same time, the 1890s, down there on the Centre, you can't see it from here, they're erecting a statue to Edward Colston, whose claim to fame was that he was responsible for the misery and deaths of a hundred thousand black people, and he gave a portion of his loot to schools in the city. Just what kind of bad faith was infecting the Bristol powers-that-be at the end of Queen Victoria's reign, that's what I wonder."

Charlotte replies, "No one is going to argue with you that the slave trade wasn't evil, but it's worth remembering the context. The English villains, like Colston, were tapping into a trade that had already been going on for centuries, though on nothing like the massive, profit-hoarding scale of Colston and his like. African chiefs used to sell their people to the Moors, in the north of Africa, and they simply regarded the Europeans as a welcome new market arriving. It wasn't just the English, the Portuguese and the Spanish and even Denmark were at it. And you don't need telling that ancient Greece, which we celebrate as the fount of civilisation, depended on slavery. Liverpool was at least as guilty as Bristol, and London was coining it, but for some reason we stigmatise ourselves as the guilty city. The question is why it took so long for people everywhere to recognise the horror of it. People in countries that thought themselves good Christians. Christians, pah! To quote your Dad."

Charley nods. "And when it was all stopped the government raised a massive loan, which we're still paying off, to recompense – the slave owners! You couldn't make it up. Those ancient Greeks couldn't have come up with a play as savage as that story. You'd have to put it on the bookshelf for comedy, not tragedy. Comedy blacker than a black hole."

"And just over there," she says, "the other side of the hill, is the Georgian House, where another big-time slaver lived, John Pinney. And do you know, he sponsored Wordsworth. The great liberal-minded William Wordsworth, just back from the French Revolution, was supported by slaving money."

"And his best mate, Coleridge, was a junkie."

"What a pair, to have launched the Romantic movement in England. Right here in Bristol."

"They both became reactionaries when they were older," Charley says. "They set the bad example that people tell you always happens, revolutionary in your youth, but a crusty old Tory when you're older. It won't happen to me, I promise you."

"I don't think it will. Your brain's going to go on buzzing in your grave. Did you never think of going to university?"

"No one did, where I grew up." He points again. "Over there. I can't say it bothers me much. What you said about Oxford the other day rang true to me. I'd chafe against all the syllabuses and stuff. I like finding my own way, even if it does mean I'm not likely ever to get a good job."

They walk down the hillside to the ponds. "Well," Charlotte says, "we've had a lively seminar. I wasn't expecting it. Shall we have a conversation next?"

"Sure. Tell me what you were expecting. Did you have a game plan for this meeting?"

"No, not at all. I don't make plans like that. I like to take things as they arise. All I was expecting was to tell you what my friend Joanna said when I asked her about Jack, as you wanted me to. She works in accounts at the firm."

"And what did she tell you?"

"Not a lot, I'm afraid. She said Jack was popular in the firm, and everyone was sad when he got the push, along with that odious little man Wheen. It was all kept hush-hush, at senior level, about the reason for it, but word has gone around that they had been forging signatures on wills. Not to steal money, probably – they would have had to alter the will itself for that – but simply to save themselves time and trouble on the probate process, which Joanna says can be a real drag."

"And is it right, as Elira believes, that your father did what he could to defend them?"

"You'd have to ask him that question. I couldn't. But it wouldn't surprise me. He's a dry old stick, but he has a strong belief in loyalty, and he could well have felt loyalty to Jack, at least. They were golfing companions, after all."

"And so might he have taken an interest in helping Jack set up his new business, the luxury goods one where I work for Elira now?"

She shrugs. "Perhaps. They could have talked about it when they were playing golf. But I'm not sure. If the thing about wills was true, my father would have disapproved of behaviour like that, so despite his loyalty he would have been chary of any business involvement with Jack."

"Thank you, Charlotte."

"Does that help? I warned you I couldn't get much from Joanna."

"It does help. There are things going on around Elira that I'd like to understand better, though they're not strictly any of my business. You've just slotted another piece into the jigsaw for me."

"Good."

"And in return I'll tell you who should really be commemorated on top of Brandon Hill. A hermit called Reginald, who lived in some sort of cave up there in the 15th century – "

She interrupts him. "Dwelt in some sort of cave. Hermits dwell, Charley, they don't live in places."

He gives her a little bow of acknowledgment. "It may be that he chose to dwell here in reverence to Saint Brendan, after whom the hill's named. Saint Brendan, yes? Irish monk, sixth century. The Irish would have you believe he sailed to discover America, to spread the good news about Jesus."

"But no one has yet discovered the farther shore of what the Irish would have us believe."

"Though they do know how to breed horses, you'll concede that?"

"Oh yes, gladly."

"And they've bred a decent writer or three, in their time."

"Ah sure they have."

"Flann O'Brien for one."

"Who?"

"Flann O'Brien. You've never heard of him? Shame on you. I'll tell you later. First, Reginald has been waiting for us. About a thousand years after Brendan, Reginald, who had also been a sailor, would be frequently visited by a young man called Sebastian – wait for it – Sebastian Cabot. He was the only surviving son of John Cabot. Why he'd survived was because he'd chickened out of joining his father's second voyage to America, which disappeared without trace. A few years later, Sebastian, with the Cabot name to help him, was all over Europe taking the credit for having discovered North America. He was such a celebrity that he became the King of Spain's Pilot-Major. But I reckon that Reginald, who had the reputation of being a surly man, would have seen through Sebastian as a pushy teenager, and would have been well sarcastic about his celebrity later, and nowadays we are cruelly in need of people like him. Saint Reginald the Iconoclast I call him. The patron saint of puncturing the hollow nonentities who pass as celebrities. Let's have a memorial up there to Reginald."

Charlotte says, "The only bit of history I learned about Brandon Hill is that it's where the Chartists used to hold their meetings."

"Did they? Excellent. Reginald would have given them his blessing."

****

She doesn't show any disdain for his room. She likes all the books. "As someone said, they do furnish a room, don't they?" In the hope that they would wind up there, he had tried to make it tidy, but had she wetted a forefinger and run it along a shelf she might have frowned. She doesn't. Not that kind of woman. They eat the pizzas and drink the Côtes du Rhône he had bought on the way, and get into his bed with no more fuss than if they had done it a hundred times before, not once. He enjoys her hands on him, as intelligent and forthcoming as her speech, and she sighs, with contentment he hopes. "You will come to my wedding, won't you?" she asks.

"Of course. I'd like to meet your boyfriend. Vivian, isn't it?"

"Well remembered."

"Oh, I've said it many times to myself, with expletives."

"Expletives?"

"I envy him his luck."

"Don't, Charley. Envy is an acid. It will burn you out."

"I've got it under control, don't worry. I know I could never be the husband for you."

"You don't know enough about horses."

"I do know a bit. Enough that Elira is taking me to Royal Ascot in a week's time, to mark her card for her, tell her what to put her money on."

"That's not knowing about horses."

"I'd love it if I could persuade her to invite you, too."

"No thanks. I've told you I don't like racing."

"But this isn't over fences, it's on the flat. They almost never get hurt."

"The jockeys use whips."

"Yes, they do."

"You've reminded me, I've got something to give Elira, a tartan sash for the dancing. I never use it. It would look as though I were taking it all mega-seriously, and the fact is I've almost stopped going, especially with Vivian coming back, so I might not be seeing her. If I give to you to pass on to her, would that be okay?"

"Sure. No problema."

"I see you've got a rack of CDs there. Shall we have some music?"

"What would you like?"

"You wouldn't have any Schubert, would you?"

"Not in my hemisphere, I'm afraid. How about Dire Straits?"

"All right. But promise me something, Charley Midsomer. One day buy yourself Schubert's piano sonata in B flat, and let it remind you of me."

"I will. Promise. B flat."

17

ELIRA IS DRIVING to Ascot. "But," she tells Charley, "you do the drive back. You're the designated driver, so just one drink. I'll need more than one."

"Okay." He is not talking. He is studying the form in the Racing Post, and, with his eyes still on the paper, thinking through what she had said as they left her house.

"I hope you'll enjoy the races," she'd said. "I don't expect you will get much social enjoyment out of it. There will be little conversation in English. But I will try to find out what I can about those people who were following you the other day. Someone there should have some suspicion."

In her dead husband's suit.he feels himself a fraud. Very well, he reckons, I'll play a part. What part can he dream up? They'll all know his real part, Elira's dogsbody, but the one before him had been Wheen, with another part on his c.v., a solicitor, so Charley could choose to be – what? A professional gambler? A dissolute aristocrat? Lord Lucan's brother, fallen on hard times? An actor, even? One who is often out of work and in need of income. I'm between parts, he thinks that's the jargon. He could enjoy this. And he's confident he's got the winner of the opener, the Jersey Stakes, over seven furlongs, for three-year-olds: Blue Jazz, from a French trainer, he wouldn't be sending it over for a holiday, it's won twice over the trip, likes the good to firm it will meet today, 13/2, French horses are usually a point or two longer than they should be on account of patriotic Brit money, second rated in the paper, it's the punt.

As they walk across the grass in the Ascot car park, Elira hands him five twenty-pound notes. "There you are, Charley, my stakes. You put them on for me. At the end of the day, if there's anything over a hundred pounds left I'll split it 50/50 with you, okay?"

"You're on."

Up in the box, Zamir, in a dark suit, greets them, and introduces them to the other five men already there. Charley can't memorise all the names, Italian, Albanian, maybe, but supposes it is not going to matter, he is not expecting conversations. All of them are smartly suited. Three have well-cut, shiny black hair, the other two are bald, one of them bearded. They all shake hands warmly, with smiles and musical mutterings, and it feels as though he is watching a room in which everybody, by tacit agreement, is wearing a face-shaped mask.

A waitress asks them what they would like to drink, and are they ready for lunch? Waiting on a long side-table is a buffet of salmon, prawns, chicken, skewered meatballs, bowls of salad, hummus with dips, summer fruits, cream, several cheeses. Bottles of red and white wine are already uncorked, half a dozen bottles of champagne await, glasses glint. A man in a racecourse uniform is collecting money and noting down bets. Charley tells Elira he will go down to the ring and do his own betting.

He is about to do so when there are new arrivals, two women and two men. One of the women is a pretty brunette in a peacock-blue silk frock over white fishnetted legs and white high heels. She opens her arms wide to greet Elira as though she is congratulating her on an Oscar, with shrieks of hilarious surprise and embraces. Elira introduces her to Charley. "Agnesa, this is Charley, who works with me. Charley, meet my friend since childhood, Agnesa."

Agnesa has a racecard, and is excited. "Look, I have just seen, in the first race there is a horse named Hebe's Blackbird. Hebe – my grandmother's name! I must put on a bet." Her voice is accented, Albanian, Italian, Montenegrin, who's counting?

"Charley is about to go and do our bets," Elira says. "Could you do one for Agnesa too?"

"Sure, How much?"

Agnesa takes a twenty-pound note from her handbag, which is discreetly branded Michael Kors, and hands it to him.

Elira asks, "Do the same bet for us, please, will you, Charley?"

"I've already picked out another horse for us. I thought that was my job."

"It is, it is, but this is a special case. I want to keep company with Agnesa."

"So that you're not jealous when I win," Agnesa chuckles.

Charley shrugs. "Okay."

In the ring, he sees that Hebe's Blackbird is 25/1 everywhere. He frowns. He'll be betting like an amateur. The bookie will have to hide a grin. Oh well, he'll do it each-way for them, to give them a squeak of a chance of money back. He puts twenty pounds each-way on it, and a tenner on Blue Jazz, which is only 11/2, less than the paper had predicted, but never mind, better a short-price winner than a long-shot loser.

Back up in the box, he watches Blue Jazz track the leader. At half-way the leading jockey's arms are already at work, Blue Jazz is going easily. Hebe's Blackbird is in a pocket on the rails, with half-a-dozen in front of it. At the two-furlong pole, the jockey pulls it out wide and with a surprising finishing burst it goes past the field and beats Blue Jazz a length. The crowd in the stands are mostly quiet, but Elira and Agnesa are defying gravity. "How much have we won?" Agnesa asks.

Charley glances at the betting slip. "Including your stake money back you get three hundred and twenty quid each of you."

The two women are holding hands and dancing. The fascinator on Agnesa's white hat quivers to the rhythm. The men watch them with indulgent smiles, before returning to quiet, intense conversation, with gesturing hands, in which Zamir appears to be central. Charley is trying to remember his grandmother's name, as he goes down to collect from the bookie. Ada, he says to himself. If there's anything called Ada going, Enchilada or something would do, I'll demonstrate my scorn of superstitious punting by sticking twenty quid of Elira's dosh on it. Back in Dunkerry Road, when he was growing up, there was a neighbour called Doris who always hoped to find a horse in the Grand National with Red in its name. She must have done all right in the days of Red Alligator, Red Rum (three times), and Red Marauder. He doesn't remember that Doris had a branded handbag, though.

When he hands Agnesa her £320, she takes his elbow and leads him out to the balcony. She is holding a flute of champagne. "A quiet word with you," she says. Charley looks back into the box, hoping he is not about to be shot by the man she had arrived with. "You are working with Elira?" she asks.

"That's right."

"And you are very good friends?"

He can see where this is going. "Just colleagues," he tells her, "just colleagues. It's business, that's all. Her business." What has happened to the actor part he had intended to play? Never mind. He likes this woman, though she is a Maserati to his Mini. She has a chuckle in her voice.

"Business, yes," she says. "What do you do for her? What is your business skill?"

"To tell you the truth, I still don't know what I want to be when I grow up. For now I'm her delivery man, and sort of consultant."

She nods. Consultant was a well-chosen word. "Tell me, is it good for you, working with her?" Her eyes are trying to read his. There is something she will share with him.

"I can't complain. She pays me well enough, and the work's not hard."

"No, I mean her, Elira. Is she difficult?"

"Not with me. She has some difficult problems with the business."

"But – she doesn't blame you for them?"

"No. I try to help her with them. Why do you ask?"

She makes a little hum. "Before, with Jack – you knew Jack?"

"No. He had died before I met her."

"With Jack, oh – the problems. He told me, it was always his fault."

"You were good friends with Jack?"

"Well, he needed somebody to talk to about her. And I'd known her since we were children, so – I told him, she has always had a – what do you say?"

"A temper?"

"Yes, a temper. Even when we were still girls. Whatever we were doing, she had to be the top bitch. Once she pulled hairs out of my head because of some silly argument we were having." Gazing out across the course, she leans her elbows on the balcony rail, which exposes her dainty cleavage below his eyes. "And the worst thing Jack told me was that they had had some terrible scene over a deal he had made that went wrong, and he wanted to make it better with her so he bought her a very expensive painting, at Christie's, but it only made her more mad, all that money he'd spent – on a picture! I felt so sorry for him, poor Jack, when he told me that story. He was just trying to please her, you know? After that, I think he gave up." Her eyes are reading his again. "Or perhaps she did."

He is moving pieces in the jigsaw that he'd thought were in place. He needs time on his own. "I must sort out a bet on the next race," he tells her, a bet that he'd sorted out on the M4.

"Nice to have had a quiet word with you, Charley. You understand?"

"I understand," he lies.

"For your own good." She gives his arm a little squeeze and they go back inside.

His selection in the second race finishes tenth. In the third it's obvious that the hot favourite, Inzaman, will stroll home, but at 10/11 it's against his principles to bet on it so he flutters on something at 33/1 that duly comes in where he used to finish in the school's annual cross-country race around Victoria Park. The next is the Hunt Cup. He has never found the winner of it, though his father used to boast that he had once got the winner at 40/1, and tipped it to a friend, doubling his risk. Charley's choice preserves his own record. In the fifth his fancy gives them a shout in the last furlong, but is overtaken by two others. He counts Elira's remaining cash. His shrewdness has so far cost her £90 of the £100 stake she had entrusted to it, but the winnings from Agnesa's grandmother mean that he is still holding £330. The last race is a listed handicap for three-year-old fillies over a mile, a reliable get-out for the bookies. Chagrined by his failures, but whipped up by his encounter with Agnesa, he defiantly slaps £50 on Lyrical Lydia at 6/1. She is fighting for her head at the start, but the jockey gets her settled after two furlongs, times her run in the straight perfectly, and wins going away. Elira gives Charley a hug, a thing she has never done before, brought on by cash and the wine she has been drinking all afternoon. He has £680 in his pocket, £290 of it coming his way. Wait till Mike hears about this.

Elira tilts the passenger seat back and tells him to wake her up when they get home.

18

AND SHE DOES spend the two-hour drive back to Bristol asleep. Charley spends it telling himself it is no concern of his whether she had any part in the death of her husband, as Agnesa had hinted. He is sick of the shadow play around the lives and deaths of others, people who are not his people. He would rather pass the M4 tedium thinking about the shape of Agnesa's peacock-blue silk dress. What did her parting squeeze of his arm say? It would be no puzzle to decode it had she grown up in England, but does it translate from Albanian? Will he ever see her again? It would be pretty to think so, but probably risky, given the milieu she inhabits. In any case, there is nothing he can do about it. So he drives, past one illuminated blue sign after another, until he pulls up at Elira's house.

He has to go in with her, to take off the borrowed suit and put his own clothes on. She takes him into her bedroom, where he had changed this morning, and asks him, "I need to do a line, do you want one with me?"

"I won't, thanks."

She leaves the room and is back, in a peignoir, before he has dressed again. He is standing in his y-fronts and socks in front of the bed. "You look ridiculous," she says, and pushes him back flat on his back. She removes his socks and pants, sheds her peignoir, and throws herself down on top of him.

He does not resist her. When, later, he wonders why not, he cannot refine out the mixture in him of courtesy to a woman, deference to his boss, and lust. The element of lust is not potent. He has always thought her mouth sensuous, and her naked body is in good shape, but there has never been affection between them, never shared laughter, and without that you can make the sex work, but you will wind up feeling lonely. He does make it work, but it is not easy, because she is at him like a puma, jumping him, withdrawing, prowling, jumping again, growling. It is like nothing he has known before. There is something desperate in her. He feels obliged to keep himself going until she will have had enough, is satisfied, but is not sure he will be able to judge it when it happens. He just wants it to stop, but that is up to her. The coke she has snorted might last half an hour. To trick his mind, it is on Agnesa he concentrates. He shuts out the memory of Charlotte, too precious to sully. When he ejaculates it brings him no pleasure.

She stops, and rolls onto a pillow, facing away from him. For a minute he does nothing, then feels he owes it to her to put an arm around her shoulder, nervous that he might be starting it up again. She just sighs, in her throat, ambiguously. Then she turns to face him. She doesn't look frustrated. Maybe he has served her needs. He doesn't know her any better than he had before. She says, "Don't go yet. I'll have trouble getting to sleep. Let's talk for a bit."

"Okay. What about?"

She sucks a tooth. "Two of those men in the box today were from Foggia. And two of them Neapolitans. Zamir can be very proud of himself to have got them there together, speaking to each other. They all said they understand the need for an agreement. Actually, the word they used would translate as 'pact', which is worrying. It would include the Albanian dealers, the Kosovars, the Italian shippers, etcetera etcetera. That's what they said. We will see, won't we?"

"We will, no doubt. But have we learned who it is who has been following me?"

"Zamir did raise the question, but everyone there said oh no, not us, not us. Possibly it is some other rogue traders. Kids, even. They get out of control, some of those kids."

"And might it be the same people who have been gazumping clients from you?"

She shrugs. "It could be. They'd have a motive. It would have been nice if we could have resolved all these questions, and consolidated our industry, but that was not to be expected. Zamir's hope is that the day will at least have increased trust by a point or two, now that people have seen each other's faces."

"There could be other groups not on his invitation list."

"Of course, of course. He knows that. The situation is always a fluid one."

"And meanwhile?"

"What can we do?" she answers. "Just keep on doing business, and hope it will all calm down."

"I wouldn't have a big bet on that."

"Zamir couldn't do more than he has done. He is good to me."

They lay quiet. Then Charley stretches. "Well, I should be getting home."

"All right. I wouldn't want you to fall asleep and Roze to find you here in the morning. She always comes in with a cup of tea for me."

"Right. I'll push off now."

He is putting his clothes on when she asks him, "By the way, what were you and Agnesa talking about, out on the balcony?"

Ah. So that's what this night has been about. "Oh," he tells her, "just the crowds, and the fashions. I showed her where the royal box is. She'd never heard of Royal Ascot until this morning, so I filled in a bit of the tradition for her. That man she came with, was that her husband?"

"No, She used to be married, but not any more. I'm surprised you didn't ask her that question yourself, at the time."

"It would have felt a bit nosey of me. A bit too personal, you know? I wanted to avoid that. I am a bloke, after all."

"Aren't you just? Have you seen any more of Charlotte, the girl you were talking to at the Scottish dancing?"

"Funny you should ask. We did have a drink the other day. Oh, that reminds me. She's got a tartan sash that she thought you might like to have."

"How nice of her. Tell her to bring it next time we're dancing."

"No, that's the point. She's not sure she'll be going much any more, because her boyfriend is coming back from Trinidad soon, and she said it would be a pity to waste the sash."

"Well then, why doesn't she give it to you to bring here for me?"

"I don't know if I'll see her again any time soon."

"Then give her my address and she can post it to me. Or better, she can bring it over herself, so that I can thank her."

"Right. I'll pass it on."

I'll pass it on very soon, he thinks as he walks home under the waxing crescent moon, because it will be an excuse to ring Charlotte.

****

He is tired the next day, after Ascot and Elira. His mood darkens when he sees, in his wing mirror, the silver Audi tracking him again. He tries going slowly, but they do the same. He tries braking sharply, but they have kept enough distance, and go past him, and will be waiting ahead. He should have done it when there was a side road into which he could dive and find a detour. In the next side road, there they are, waiting. He makes a note of their registration. If he rings the DVLC, will they disclose the owner's name and address? Probably not, confidential, sorry. Pretty please? That won't cut any ice. Civil service ice is unyielding. What is it they are after? Daily patterns make no sense, there are none. Today it's Bath, Melksham, and St Andrew's, back in Bristol. Elira's theory, that it's intimidation, is more plausible, and it's working. They surely can't be logging addresses he calls at, Wheen will have supplied them. He thinks of calling on Wheen, who lives close to St Andrew's, and throttling him for an answer, but he knows what the answer would be, there is simply nothing Wheen can do about it, it is quite out of his hands, so sorry, cup of Earl Grey? Suppose he crawls up to traffic lights until they switch to red, then jumps out and confronts them? They'd just sneer him away. No arguing with their sort. And apparently Zamir can't answer for them. They must come from a different tribe from the ones he allegedly reconciled yesterday.

He tells Mike about it in the pub.

"It's an occupational hazard you'll just have to live with," Mike answers. "You chose the occupation."

"That's all the help I get for buying the first round?" He's told Mike about Ascot, so felt obliged to fork out.

"Short of going to the cops, which for obvious reasons you're not going to consider," Mike says, "the only recourse I can suggest is that tomorrow I track behind them in my burger van and give them a rear-end shunt, and you pay for any damage."

"Trouble with that is that they're not there every day."

"Well, give me a ring next time they are and if I'm not in a complicated burger transaction I'll be there for you."

"It is a nice idea," Charley admits. "But the odds are we'll be miles out of Bristol and you'd never find us."

Their brows unfurrow when two of their old school friends come into the pub, and spot them. "Charley's buying," Mike tells them. "He's flush after a good day at Royal Ascot."

"Right, then, mine's a pint of Butcombe," says Don, who works as an aerospace fitter.

"Make it a Guinness for me," says Bazza, a security guard.

"And two chasers," Don adds. "You deserve a proper celebration."

Charley buys the drinks. When he gets them back to the table, Bazza – his parents had named him Basil but with that name he would not have survived in the playground – is boasting that his uniform gets him into any match he fancies at Ashton Gate. "Even when I'm not on duty. They never ask."

"How about you, Chas?" Don asks. "What you up to these days?"

"Deliveries," Charley tells him.

"What, Amazon is it? DHL? Sainsos?"

"No, it's a private company I work for, exclusively."

"Ooooh," Bazza joshes, "exclusive are we?"

"Delivering what?" Don asks.

Charley catches Mike's eye, and trusts him not to blab. "Luxury goods," he says.

"Lacy underwear?" Bazza suggests.

"No, it's foodstuffs." He wants to change the subject. "How are things in aerospace?" he asks Don.

"We're flying," Don answers.

The bants go on, with more rounds, until Bazza asks, "Did you hear about Frankie Whittle?"

"What about him?" Mike replies. "Don't tell me he's stopped being an eejit."

"Oh, he has," Bazza says. "He's stopped all right. I went to his funeral last month."

"What?" Mike says. "He's died?"

"Well, I hope so, since he's ashes now. A stroke was the official line, but, no, he'd been on drugs, heavy. I talked to his sister at the funeral, and she said he'd always been fooling around with drugs, but it got big time when his marriage went bust. Poor bugger."

Again, Charley is catching Mike's eye, but he trusts their friendship. Mike can be an acerbic berk when it is just the two of them, but in company he is remarkably good at keeping shtum. Good old reliable Mike. He's lightening up the conversation now by telling them about panelling he's putting in for a neighbour. "She saw what I'd done in my own place, and asked me to do it for her too. Trouble is, I have to charge her more than I'd like just for the materials. You seen the price now of tongued and grooved pine? No wonder they're all doing so well in Norway, so I read in the paper."

Don says, "I don't know that life is that expensive in Norway."

"Maybe not," Mike answers. "Life might be cheap there for all I know. It's wood, their wood, that's expensive."

Norwegian wood. Lying in his bed, a tad sozzled, Charley grins as he sings it, quietly. He'll ring Charlotte tomorrow.

19

SHE IS NOT in her usual sunny mood. They take a walk around the old dockside, at her suggestion, and for a while she says little. For him it is a place of happy memories, seamen throwing oranges from their cargo boat to a gang of kids, him a little one of them. He tries to brighten her up. He gestures at the activities on the harbour now, rowing-club boats, kayaks, paddle boards, windsurfers, ferries, and says, "Would you believe, when the docks stopped as an industry here, because container ships were taking over, thirty or forty years ago, the council had plans to concrete over it all, for motorists? It took a packed Town Meeting in the Colston Hall to tell them to think again. My Dad was there. That was the mentality of the council then. Bone-heads. And those magnificent mobile cranes over there, they were going to scrap. Look at it now."

She is nodding, but says nothing beyond a grunt of acknowledgment.

"What's up?" he asks.

She sighs.

"Your boyfriend's back soon from Trinidad, isn't he? I thought you'd be humming with impatience."

"Where do I start?" she replies.

"Is it something I did wrong?"

"It's nothing to do with you, Charley. It's my father. I told them yesterday that Viv and I are going to get married in November, and I can't believe his response. He said, 'You are proposing to present us with khaki grandchildren?' Oh, I knew he wasn't happy about my going out with Viv, but it turns out he had been assuming it was one more regrettable aberration in my life, and that one day he would be proudly approaching the altar with his virginal daughter on his arm and delivering her to some nice white accountant. Giving me away – that's the phrase, isn't it? As though I were his precious property. He'd even got the right man for me lined up, a Scotsman of course, son of a friend of his. Invited them down to visit us regularly."

"Jeez. What did you say?"

"He didn't give me time to say anything to him. That was his exit line. He stormed out, slamming the door behind him. I haven't seen him since. He had supper in his study."

"Your mother, what did she say to you?"

"Oh, she was full of maternal sympathy, of course. But she wouldn't dream of questioning his attitude. She never has. She's just put up with it, all these years. I don't know what she thinks. She doesn't say. Doesn't dare. Poor thing."

"Will your brother stick up for you?"

"No chance. He got a good physics degree at Strathclyde and took it straight into the insurance business. A job with another old school friend of my father's. What a waste. And now of course there are two sweet white grandchildren up in Edinburgh, and my father has set up trust funds for them. Oh, Charley, if you only knew the depths of misery behind our smartly painted front door."

"I don't know what I can say. Except, you can count on me, for the rest of your life."

"That is a lovely thing to hear. Thank you. I'm sorry to unload all that on you, but it was only yesterday. I'm still trying to stomach it. I feel better for having shared it."

They walk silently, past the modern blocks of flats still being extended on the harbour's north side. She nods at them. "They're not too bad, are they?"

"I'd call them harmless, at best. When you think of the Victorian brick monsters that used to be there, the gas works for example, it was like a giant sculpture of the city's industrial history. England's history. Ugly, sure, but – And now. I heard an architect describe this kind of thing as pixie shit."

"You're an old romantic, you are."

"I know. I can't change that."

"Don't even try."

"Bristol was so lucky to have attracted Brunel here. It was pure chance, you know. He came here, for the first time, to convalesce, after the Thames Tunnel fell in on him, that he was helping his father build, and while he was here it happened that they announced a competition to design a bridge over the river at Clifton, and, well, you know the rest. From then on he was in love with Bristol, even though the city fathers were always stingy about financing his projects. The railway down from London, the s.s.Great Britain over there, look at it, and another ship before that, the Great Western, and a hotel for the railway passengers going on to New York, the Underfall Yard, and… Reasons to be cheerful on a grim day for you."

"Shall we have a cup of tea and a nice cake? On me."

In the café, he asks her, "Are you going to tell Vivian what your father said?"

"Eventually."

"He needs to know what he's getting into."

"I don't think he has many illusions about that. We've already had conversations about my parents."

"I guess Vivian is descended from the indentured labourers they took over there from India?"

"Yes. Bihar is where his forefathers came from. Indenture was a shade better than slavery."

"Only a shade, from what I've read about the system."

"At least it was a choice. The poverty in colonial India was dreadful, and they escaped it. His grandparents must have been go-getters, because the family have become significant in Trinidad. One of his uncles is in Parliament there. His Dad is a successful businessman."

"So your kids will get their trust funds."

"We'll see."

"You'd have thought your father might have been impressed by a family like that."

"Yes. But they've got brown skin."

Charley sighs. What is there to say?

"Viv has told me there's race distinctions in Trinidad. It's not brutal, like in the U.S.A., it's more like the caste system, back in India. Not racism, but classism, rather. The lighter brown people think themselves superior to the darker ones."

"What is it about the human race...?"

"He says he can see something of that in his own mother. She was clicking her tongue when he was going out with a girl there who was darker than they are."

"It's viral. Where does it spring from, this kneejerk assumption that whiter is better?"

"Viv told me that Montezuma was a pale Aztec."

"Is it something Freud could explain? Maybe he does, I haven't read much of him. Is it that brown is the colour of dung, so to be avoided for fear of infection?"

"But it's also the colour of this table," she says. "And this tea."

"And this delicious-looking chocolate on your cake."

"Hands off."

"And that lovely girl's hair over there. And autumn leaves."

"And my horse, Jasper. Brown is gorgeous."

"You might make a case that it's colonialist guilt, but Viv's mother puts that one to bed."

"I think it's simply that everybody has insecurity about their own worth, so they need some evidence that they are worthier than others, and visual evidence is readily available, so being white is like an officer's ribbons."

"So, vanity. Is it one of the seven deadlies?"

"No, but pride is."

"Not quite the same thing. Pride is sometimes justifiable."

"I reckon it was for reasons like this, or unreasons, that our lot wiped out the Neanderthals. They didn't have to. Surely there was enough mammoth to go around."

"It is a shame," Charley says. "They were pretty good guys, those Neanderthals. They'd have won a fair number of Olympic golds if they'd survived. And Nobel prizes, possibly. They had bigger brains than we have."

"But could they speak? In order to accept the award, and thank everybody who had contributed to it?"

"We can't know. But I don't believe they could have lived

together for 360,000 years without saying a word to each other."

"My parents have."

He nods. "I sometimes have this thought, that a billion years from now there will be a quite different breed of intelligent beings inhabiting the planet, and to them, to their archaeologists and anthropologists, what they can piece together about the human race, here billennia before them, will look like a brief flash in the pan, before it wiped itself out, and things returned to a prehistoric state, and evolution started to come up with whatever their new breed is."

"What will it be, do you think?"

"I don't think about it. I'm not into science fiction."

"Oh." Charlotte reaches into her bag. "Here's the tartan sash I thought I'd give to Elira. Will you take it for her?"

"I meant to tell you, I mentioned it to her, and she was pleased, and said she'd prefer it if you could deliver it to her yourself, so that she can say thankyou. She'd like to see you again."

"All right. Where does she live?"

"I'll take you, next time we meet. Not today. Today I want to be greedy for your time. With Viv coming back, I know you'll think me the old romantic, but there's something I want to tell you... "

"Stop," she says. "You're talking like a train coming out of a tunnel, and I know what the guard's van will look like."

"Don't worry, I'm resigned. You can't marry everybody you fall in love with."

"No. Look what it would cost you in wedding cake."

As they rise to leave, she says, "You have cheered me up."

"The guard's van, you mean?"

"No, all of it. The whole damn train. Thank you."

****

Drive the fork down at an angle, turn the soil, and collect some half-a-dozen small Charlottes into the canvas bag his landlord has supplied. I dig Charlotte, he grins to himself. Two hours of this, then weeding, knocks sixteen quid off his rent for the week. The blackberries are already fruiting – they seem to come earlier every year – and those he puts in a plastic bag for himself. He's not giving them to that miserable sod waiting in the hall, he'll have them for supper with Madagascar vanilla custard.

He enjoys it here, on Redland Green, on top of the hill. Steve, the ambulance driver, once told him, "Know what I loves about Bristol? It's like Rome."

"Go on."

"Built on seven 'ills it is, like Rome is."

Near the allotments is a playground chirping with children, and beside it a bowls club, where properly dressed elderly men wearing ties and ribboned straw hats weigh the wood and squint at the line they fancy. He might take up that game one day. On the other side of the allotments, beyond the brook down in the little wooded valley, is the Dingle, where people throw balls for their dogs. Next to the Georgian church, which Pevsner commended, is a posh tennis club, and on the green itself a man-sized sarsen stone. It is what is called an erratic, a rock that doesn't belong here geologically. Who sweated to drag it up here, like a singular Stonehenge? Some say it was a boundary stone for the Roman soldiers on their route march from Bath to their port down at Sea Mills, but it has been here much longer than that. It is a mystery, which is why Charley likes it.

As he forks and harvests and weeds, he can't help thinking again about what Charlotte's father had said to her. What can it have been like in that law practice, with a bigot like McFinn, and the scared liar Wheen, and Jack, ready to switch to dealing drugs?

In the pub that evening, he tells Mike about it.

"Sounds like they had all bases covered," Mike remarks, "in the frailties their clients were presenting them with."

"Doctors don't need to have had all the diseases they diagnose."

"Lawyers are different. Their job is to find ways round things, not cure them."

"Same as politicians."

"Right," Mike says. "Why do you suppose half the MPs at Westminster have got law degrees? A problem comes up, they don't look for how to fix it but for how to dodge it. That's why they're called Conservatives, including quite a few in Labour."

"We ought to start a new party called the Cynics. But it wouldn't work. The ancient Greeks tried that, but none of them would believe a word of what the others were saying."

"Reminds me of that old joke about some toff saying, 'I say, old boy, we're starting a new club called the Apathetics, do you fancy joining? No? Oh well, it doesn't really matter.'"

"There's a party in Dublin that would be just right for us," Charley says. "Fianna Fail Better."

"Sign me up."

20

ELIRA TELLS HIM she has been auditing the books, "and we are eight per cent down on the year compared to last year."

He can already see where this will be heading. He'll clean his paint brushes.

"You do lose clients of course for all sorts of reasons," she continues. "Some move away, some fall foul of the law, some die, a few kick their habit, I suppose, but in the past we have had fresh clients to make up for the missing ones. I've told all of them, the loyal ones, that I'm cutting the price of coke by fifteen per cent, and I'm trying to make up for it, from our point of view, by modest nudges on the price of other goods. I've done what I can to locate new clients. I've even been giving thought to some kind of bonus scheme – recruit a new client for us and receive a commission. But the plain hard fact is that we are still eight per cent down, and it could mean accepting a gradually increasing deficit."

"So you're working towards telling me that I've got to accept a pay cut."

"No, no. What I want you to do is go and speak to a few more defaulters, see what you can find out about why they're not buying any more. Like you did once before."

Roze comes in. Elira glances at Charley and puts her finger to her lips. Roze tells her mother she's going over to see her friend Amy. "I'll be back for supper."

Roze leaves, and Elira resumes. "Because orders never will be regular – it's not like a monthly subscription – it's been difficult for me to identify permanent defaulters, people who have presumably been hijacked by some rival outfit, but I've made a short list, just three or four, of people I had reason to count on as loyal clients, people I've known personally, who have not sent me an order in the past three months. I want you to go and find out why not."

"If you know them personally, wouldn't it be better if you went and asked them yourself?"

"I've always avoided personal contact with them since they became clients because it could be embarrassing for them, and also they might worry about being compromised legally. A meeting could serve as evidence if a case were ever to go to court. Sticking to online business guarantees some protective confidentiality. There are of course one or two I do see in the normal course of events, at the Scottish dancing for instance, but neither they nor I would dream of mentioning our business arrangements."

"Okay, let me have the list," Charley says, "and I'll give it a try, but my gut instinct is that it might not yield any more info than it did last time."

"Maybe not, but we've got to try something. I'm doubtful whether what Zamir did with his Ascot day will have gone to the heart of the problem. There are other players in the game. Dark players. Different rules."

Intriguing, he thinks later, that she didn't even mention how the Ascot day had ended. As though it had been no more than a passing amusement. Well, that suits him. He has no wish to remember it, still less to repeat it, and prays that she has not added it to his job description.

He calls at the four addresses on Elira's defaulters list. Two of them tell him it is none of his business, one is more aggressive in advising him to get lost, but a fourth is more forthcoming. A man about the same age as he is, living in a flat overlooking the Avon Gorge, he invites Charley in for a drink. "What do you fancy?"

Charley eyes the array of bottles lined up on a low stone shelf, and replies, "A whisky?" He notices that his host, James, pours him a Johnny Walker rather than one of the single malts he can see, and pours himself a glass of claret.

"How can I help you?" James asks.

Charley remembers to bring the bottle of Côtes de Nuits from his bag, and hands it to him. "Elira presents her compliments, and wonders if you want to remain on her client list."

James examines the label, nods, and says, "Thank you. She's noticed I haven't ordered anything from her lately?"

"Right. She hopes you got her message about a fifteen percent discount."

"Oh yes."

"But perhaps you don't want any of her goods any more?"

"Charley – that's the name, right?"

"Charley, that's me."

"I have to tell you, Charley, or tell her, rather, that a fifteen percent cut doesn't, er, cut it. I'm an investment advisor, so every day I am looking at margins and market shifts, and she ought to be talking about twenty per cent at least. That's where the market is moving."

"And you know where to get a deal at that lower rate?"

"I do. And you'll appreciate that it's a substantial saving on an expensive outlay, buying in bulk."

"Can I ask you who is offering twenty per cent off?"

"I can't give you a name. You'll understand that a degree of professional discretion is required. But what I can tell you is that it is not just the source I have located, it's the whole market that has been lowering the price. At this wholesale level, I mean, I can't say anything about street prices, that's not my field. But I have made enquiries through contacts elsewhere, not just in Bristol, and that's the going rate now. It might change again. It's a highly volatile market."

"If you can't give me a name, can you help by giving me a nationality?"

"I suppose there's no harm done if I murmur, the accent is Italian. I've never asked him where he is from. I don't mind telling you that much, if it's of any help, because I like Elira, I've met her a few times, and I wish her well. But business is business, you know?"

"Italian. You can't pin it down to a region of Italy?"

"I can't. I'm not that much of an aficionado of Italy. The south of France is my getaway of preference. I have a little place there, near Aix-en-Provence. You might like to see it one day? I'm a good cook. You'd love it, I'm sure."

"I dare say I would, but I'm not free, I'm afraid. But thank you."

"Any time. You know where to find me."

****

"Twenty per cent?" Elira exclaims.

"He says that's where the whole market has moved."

"Hm. I'll have to ask Zamir what he knows about that. Maybe

I can arrange a cut from him. Did you ask James who is supplying him? That's what we need to know."

"He wouldn't give me a name. An Italian accent is all he'd say. At least we know it's not Wheen himself."

"We knew that already."

"I did ask what region of Italy, but he couldn't identify it."

"Or wouldn't," Elira grunts. "Foggia is my guess." She is drumming her fingers.

"Oh," Charley says. "I got in touch with Charlotte and told her that you'd like it if she handed you that sash herself. I can bring her round. When would be good for you?"

She checks her order book. "There's three deliveries for you Friday. Saturday there's nothing.'

"Saturday. I'll see if she's free then."

"Teatime. She can meet Roze. She won't be at school."

****

"Let's` make a day of it," Charlotte says when he rings her. "I'll pick you up at eleven, and we can go for a pub lunch somewhere, then a walk, and back for tea with Elira. Sound good?"

"Any day with you sounds good."

"There might not be many more. Viv is back the week after next. It doesn't mean I won't be seeing anything of you. I hope you and Viv will be friends. But obviously I'll have to put him first, with the wedding coming up."

When she picks him up on Saturday she says, "How about The Druid's Arms in Stanton Drew?"

"I don't know it."

"It's excellent for lunch. You'll see. We can eat out in the garden, next to three of the famous standing stones, you know? Neolithic."

"That'll be mammoth steak and chips then."

"And a flagon of mead. No, reindeer would have been their favourite."

Over the top of Dundry they go, the Mendips rising in the distance. "I love Mendip," Charley says. "Up where you come from, the Cotswolds, it's very pretty and domestic and all, but there's something cosy about it, until you get up Cheltenham way. But that" – he gestures at the skyline – "it's muscular, you know? You get me?"

"I get you."

"You can understand why it suited them in the Stone Age. The broad sweep of it, great for hunting, plenty of caves to live in, and down to the Levels for your fish."

"Well," she says, "before them it had been tundra, in the Ice Age. A peninsula of the continent then. The ice sculpted it. That's what you love about it. Muscular sculpture."

They drive down to Chew Magna, around the cricket ground, and into Stanton Drew. In the flagstoned and oak-beamed bar of the pub she picks up a pamphlet about the stones, and out in the garden, at the back, there they are, three of the lichened stones. "After we've eaten," she says, "we go through that gateway and take a walk around the circle of standing stones over there. It's huge." She skims a glance through the pamphlet. "Yes, they've got it in here. The myth is that they were dancers at a wedding, but they'd chosen Sunday for it, tut-tut, and they were all turned to stone for their sin."

"So when was this?"

She shrugs. "Late Stone Age. Three, four thousand B.C."

"I don't think they'd invented Sunday then."

"Nor sin, probably," Charlotte says. "Though I'm not sure about that. I read somewhere that the Neolithic agricultural revolution was the worst mistake we ever made. It led to land ownership and property, and so to class, then warfare, and slavery, especially female slavery. My great-grandmother times two hundred generations was most likely kept in the back of the cave for sex and childcare and cooking."

"But they needed food," Charley says. "They could grow crops now, not rely on luck in hunting and gathering."

"Sure, she says, "and the outcome was what I've just gone on about, and the archaeologists will tell you that our average height went down about half a foot. Whereas hunter-gatherers got plenty of exercise. Good fitness."

After lunch they walk around the stone circle, and are surprised by how many of the stones have fallen flat. "They should have got the Stonehenge crew over," Charley says, "to show them how to do foundations."

"If they were dancers," she says, "some of them have had too much to drink. It can be a problem at weddings."

"You're thinking about yours."

"I have to. There'll be a lot of my family down from Scotland, and you know what they're like when it's free booze."

"Your father will keep control."

"I expect so. He's good at that."

"Has he given you more grief about Vivian?"

"Not another word. He's said his piece, his poisonous piece."

"He rests his case."

21

ROZE ANSWERS THE bell, and at once she and Charlotte are hitting it off. It turns out that Charlotte had been at the school where Roze is now, Cote Park Hall, and they are giggling at the foibles of teachers they both know. Elira and Charley talk quietly on the other side of the sitting-room, by the high windows. She tells him she has not yet managed to contact Zamir, to ask him about the market price. Then she announces, "Tea time." With Roze's help, she serves a big pot of tea, gilt-rimmed cups, saucers and plates, and a two-tiered stand of fancy cakes and macaroons.

Charlotte says, "Before we start, this is the moment for me to decorate you, Elira." She brings the tartan sash out of her bag, and puts it over Elira's shoulder. "My aunt in Perth gave it to me, but I don't think I'll be dancing with you for some time now, I'm going to be too busy getting married, and it's too bonny to be left in a drawer."

Elira and Roze congratulate her, and the talk turns to the stone dancers at Stanton Drew. "It's such an atmospheric place," Charlotte says. "Easy to imagine yourself back in the Stone Age. Have you been there?"

"No," Roze says. "I've never heard of it."

"It's only a short drive over Dundry," Charlotte says. "Great views on the way."

"We'll go, on a nice day," Elira tells Roze.

"There is so much history, and mythology too," Charlotte continues. "It's all in a pamphlet I picked up. Here, I'll give it to you." She looks in her bag. "I must have left it in the car. I'll nip down and get it. Back in a minute."

While she is gone, Charley asks Roze, "How's your Spanish coming on?"

"Oh, I love it. I think it's what I might want to do at uni."

"Where do you fancy going?"

"Well, I'll try for Oxbridge, of course. But it's so competitive, I'll need a back-up option, in case. Maybe Manchester."

She is interrupted by a loud scream from the road, followed by a series of breathless shrieks.

Charley moves quickly to the window, but a big sycamore blocks the view. "I think that was Charlotte," he says. "I'd better go and see what's up." He runs downstairs, and along the path to the gate. He is in time to see the silver Audi taking off in the direction of St Michael's Hill, on screeching tyres. There is nobody on the pavement, no Charlotte, just her car, empty.

He snatches out his phone and tries her number. It rings, but no one answers. He wasn't expecting her to. He runs back into the house. Elira sees the alarm on his face, and tells Roze to go to her room.

"Where's Charlotte?" Roze asks. "What's happened?"

"Your room. Now."

Roze leaves, unwillingly.

Charley says, "It's that car that has been following me. They must have snatched her. There's no sign of her. Oh Jesus." His hands are on his temples. "We'll have to ring the police." He takes his phone out.

"No," Elira says. "Not on your phone. Nor on mine. The police will trace the number. We can't have them in here. Run to the payphone at the end of the street, up there on the right. Here – " From the hall stand she takes a fedora from the wooden peg where Jack must have left it. "Put this on. There might be CCTV coverage there. You mustn't be identified." She takes a white silk scarf from another peg. "Wrap this around your face."

He does as he's told. He is too wretched to think for himself.

He keys in 999 and asks for the police. A woman's voice answers. He tells her, "A young woman has just been kidnapped on Kingsdown Parade, and taken away in a car. It's a silver Audi. They went off toward St Michael's Hill. I can give you the registration. Hold on." In his wallet he finds the number he had noted down a week or two ago, and reads it out. "Please, this is extremely urgent. It's criminal."

"Thank you, sir. Can you – "

He hangs up. Still muffled in the scarf and hat, he pauses. If there is CCTV he'd better not go back to Elira's. He walks fast, down the hill, to the bookshop.

"What's this?" Tim asks. "Is Scorsese shooting in Bristol?"

Charley hands the fedora and scarf to Tim. "Tim, it's not funny. Something terrible has just happened. I'll tell you another time. Take these for me. Have you got a coat you could lend me?"

Tim finds him an old blue duffle coat.

"Thanks. I'll get it back to you as soon as I can."

His stomach is sobbing but he affects calm as he walks down Christmas Steps, through the Centre, and back to his room by way of Hotwells and Granby Hill, a long way round.

Charlotte must be terrified. What do those bastards want her for? As a hostage? To ransom her in return for all Elira's clients?

At home, there is a call from Elira. "You reported it to the police?"

"Yes."

"What did you tell them?"

"I told them a woman had been kidnapped on Kingsdown Parade, and I gave them details of the car. Though they've probably switched plates."

"I wish you hadn't told them where it happened.".

"For fuck's sake, Elira, I want the police to catch them. That's what matters."

"It won't help them, knowing where she was snatched. All it does is draw attention. To us."

"Her car's still there."

"Charley, I'm taking Roze away. I don't know how long for. Until this is over. A week or two, let's hope. You realise what must have happened? They must have been keeping surveillance here. All they knew from Wheen was my address, and that it's a woman running the business here. He wouldn't have given them a description of me, no need. They saw Charlotte come out and assumed she was me. I never go out on foot. She'll tell them they've got the wrong woman."

"They won't want to believe that. Even if they do, they won't care. If it's not the right woman, she'll do as a warning."

"When they find out they've missed their target, they'll be back. For me. To rub me out of the picture. Charley, it's too dangerous for me to stay here for now. I've got Roze to think about. She knows nothing. Oh god. I don't want to take any final decisions yet, until I've thought it through, and maybe Zamir could do something to help me at his end, but this could mean the end of the business. At any rate, no deliveries until you hear from me again. All right?"

"Got it."

"And you keep well away from here. Unless they find her quickly, the police will be knocking on doors along here, trying to sniff out what the game is. I hope the CCTV can't trace you back leaving my house. The neighbours know nothing. They'll get nowhere with their enquiries here. We've got to lie low. Capiche?"

"OK. What will those bastards do when they know they've made a mistake? Do with her?"

"How can I know? If we are lucky, they'll just dump her somewhere, with curses. She's no use at all to them."

Oh Jesus. Charley's eyes are shut. He doesn't want to look at this world. If we are lucky, she'd said. We.

22

RANDOLPH WHEEN HAD unleashed these dogs. He must know where to hunt them down. Charley goes over to St Werburgh's, telling himself not to throttle Wheen on sight, thumbs in his throat, not till after he's coughed up.

He finds Wheen's house in scaffolding. A middle-aged woman answers the bell.

"Is Randolph in?" Charley asks her.

"Mr Wheen, you mean? No, he's moved away. We've just bought the house. It was all done in a great rush, but we're delighted with it. As you can see we're doing… "

He interrupts her. "Have you got a forwarding address for him?"

"I'm afraid not. He said he was moving to Kenya, and would let us know later where to send his mail."

Kenya. In Wheen's mendacious mouth that could mean Brislington, or Backwell. He wouldn't want to abandon his haunts.

The county cricket ground is only a short walk away. When he gets there, Charley finds a county second eleven match in progress, with a handful of men and a dog spectating. The members' bar is open, but only a couple of lads are drinking.

He goes to the Old England. "Randolph?" the barman says. "No, I haven't seen him in here for some weeks. Not like him. People have been asking for him. I did hear he was going abroad somewhere."

So maybe he has. Done a bunk because he knew things were heating up. Charley is stumped. Then he thinks, the golf club. Which club? He is lucky at the second one he tries, but all the woman can tell him is that, yes, Mr Wheen was a member here but he resigned last month, and no, she cannot disclose any further details.

There is nothing to do but wait. Fret and wait. He rings the riding school. No, Charlotte has not shown up for work. She must be ill. He keeps on ringing her mobile number, knowing that it will not be answered. Perhaps Elira will gets news from Zamir. Meanwhile, he checks the Post and the Western Daily Press and the local radio news, but there is nothing. No alerts from the police. They have probably put it down as a domestic.

On Tuesday, he takes the bus to Stoke Bishop and does what he has been telling himself he can't do, ring the bell at Charlotte's home. Her mother answers, and, as he's feared, she is in a bad way. No, Charlotte is not in. She has been missing since the weekend. They've reported it to the police. "Who are you?" she asks.

"I'm a friend of hers."

"I've seen you before," she says. "You were at the Scottish dancing, with Elira, weren't you? Some while ago."

"Yes, I was." There is nothing more he can say.

"And would you have any idea where she could have gone? We are beside ourselves with worry. She's never done this before. She'd always tell us where she was."

"I wish I could help, but I've no idea."

"If you do hear anything from her, you will let the police know, won't you?"

"Straight away. I'm sorry to have troubled you."

She nods, with tears of anxiety in her eyes.

He shouldn't have gone there. She knows of his connection to Elira, and that could be a lead for the police. But how much suspicion would he have aroused, merely a friend calling? And the police would not be able to find Elira soon, wherever she had gone with Roze, and it will all be cleared up before she reappears in Bristol. All the same, he shouldn't have, but it was better than doing nothing, which is all he now has left to do.

On Wednesday, the Post does have three paragraphs about a missing woman, Charlotte McFinn of Stoke Bishop. Police are anxious to speak to a caller who had reported the abduction of a woman in Kingsdown on Saturday.

On Thursday, there is news, on the national front pages, and television. It is a big story. The body of a young white woman has been found in the River Avon, near Hanham Lock. Not identified yet. There are multiple stab wounds, and evidence of sexual assault.

Maybe it's not her? Things happen.

He lies on his bed, days and nights. He can't sleep. He wishes he could. Dreams, nightmares, any dreams at all would be far kinder than the images that are flaying him, over and again, and again, knotting his muscles, and will not stop. It's a brainworm. Knives driving into Charlotte's soft skin. Her cries, of fear, of pain. No one there to help her. Him not there. Their sexual assaults on her body, still alive, or dead, what does it matter? It didn't matter to them, that's not what they grabbed her for, it was a perk. This is the bottom, the very deep, of the pit of human evil.

And, inevitably, guilt crystallises. If only he had, if he had not, if only. A hundred apparently random events, innocent moves, led here How could he have known? But now he does know. Him not there. He wonders if he can hold this knowledge and yet survive. Could anybody?

On Friday, the body has been identified. Charlotte McFinn, a solicitor's daughter. Next of kin have been notified, &c. Deepest condolences to the family, &c. Dedicated team of detectives and staff working on it, extra patrols, appeal to anyone with any information, &c. &c.

Every few days he will see a news report, usually quite brief, that somebody, most often a young black man, in London most frequently, has been stabbed, or sometimes shot, to death. Usually drugs-related. Usually he can't go on reading for a while, so finds some trivial household occupation. He is losing weight, because he has no appetite.

23

HE IS WAITING for Kenny Symes. The Albert pub is busy this Saturday lunchtime, loud with weekend shoppers and Bedminster locals fuelling up for the City match down the road. Kenny hasn't got far to come from the Asda superstore where he's stacking shelves, but he's ten minutes late. Charley takes another mouthful of pale ale, which he needs for what he has to do. It is two months since Charlotte was killed, he's not heard from Elira and doesn't want to hear. He has to talk to Kenny. It matters.

The boy arrives with the expected apology about some hold-up at work. Charley asks him what he'd like to drink, and has to wait his turn to be served. When he gets back to the table with the lager, Kenny has gone. He spots him on the far side of the bar talking to two young women in Asda uniforms. Kenny catches his eye, gestures, then returns. "Sorry about that. They work where I do, but I don't get much chance to chat them up at work."

"Which one have you got your eye on?"

"Either of them would do me okay, but Sylvia, the blonde one, is engaged, so I've got more chance with Sheila, the dark one."

"You haven't got a steady, then?"

"I've got two steadies, but you need a few on the substitutes' bench, don't you?" He glances at his watch. "Mum said you wanted to talk to me about something."

"Yes. She asked me to have a word with you, when I was doing some painting for her. It's something she said your Dad would have done. I'm sorry you lost him. I'm sorry I lost my Dad, but I was older than you are. I'm not your Dad, but I've known you since you were a titch kicking a ball around in our street. so I told your Mum I'd do my best. It won't take long. It's a conversation I've had before, but I was on the receiving end then, and it was my Dad, asking me. About drugs. Your Mum's worried that you might be messing around with them."

"With drugs?"

"Yes."

"What drugs?"

Charley shrugs. "Your Mum wouldn't know, would she?"

"So why is she worried?"

"Kenny, which drugs isn't the point. I know you could find anything you wanted on the street. The point I want to make to you is that using any of them can be a gateway to something worse. I've seen it happen. It's like a whirlpool, you get a buzz swimming around the edge of it, with spice or ket or something, but you want something more, it sucks you in, sucks you down, you can't get out. It can ruin your life. And finish your life. You don't want that."

"You've seen it happen, you said?"

"I have." Charley pauses. "A bloke I'd been at school with, a year below me. He couldn't find the strength to get out. It did for him. It's a murderous place to be. People die."

"You never used, then?" Kenny asks.

"A couple of times I tried a bit of weed, nothing more. It didn't do much for me, which was lucky, because I knew I wouldn't have the strength to stop if I'd let it suck me in. I've got an addictive gene in me, I know that. I've paid a price for it in other ways, but not with drugs."

"What, then?"

"Well." Charley grins. "Girls, for one thing. The horses. But I'm not going to try to warn you off them, I've had too much fun there. Look, I've said enough. I'm no lecturer. I promised your Mum. She's a good sort. You haven't said how much you might be into it, and I'm not looking to prise a confession out of you. I'm not a priest, either. Or a cop. There's no end of things I'm not. But here you are – " He writes his number on a beer mat, and slides it to Kenny. "Ring me any time you feel in need of a good talking-to."

"Thanks, Mr Midsomer."

"I'm not Mr Midsomer, not for another twenty years. I'm Charley, right?"

"Right."

"One other thing. You ever get to see the Robins?"

"Can't afford it. I'm not a junior any more."

"Like I thought. Look, when there's a match down the Gate you fancy, give me a ring and I'll take you."

"That would be mint. But – you seen the price of seats now?"

"I know. Wicked."

"There's people I hear talking in the shop about the matches, but a lot of the time they're people with a dozen bottles of wine in their trolley, or stuff from the delicatessen counter. Like lobsters, you know? We're selling lobsters now."

Charley swallows the last of his pale ale. "I don't want to turn this into bribery," he says, "but I'll be much happier forking out for two seats if you know – you don't have to tell me – it's if you know you're not using."

"I get you."

"Good. Don't expect me to be cheering with you. It's against my beliefs."

"What do you mean?"

"Watching the City."

"Eh? You a Gashead then?"

"Right."

"Growing up in Bemmy, supporting the Filth?"

"Right. I never wanted to be like everybody else."

"You must have got done over in the playground."

"I was proud of the bruises. They were my badges of nonconformity."

Kenny is grinning, and shaking his head.

"Just so you know," Charley says.

On his way home he stops at the music shop on St George's Road and buys a CD of Alfred Brendel playing Schubert's Piano Sonata in B flat.